THINK AHEAD . . .

"Who was here? Who were you talking to?"

"Some man trying to collect from me for the Campfire Girls."

"I heard Patrick. I swear I heard Patrick."

Angus slapped her face. "I don't want to hear his name on your lips. I happen to like the fellow but he's not for you."

Fay moved to the mantel and seized a porcelain candlestick and hurled it at him.

He dodged; it smashed against the wall.

"Next time," he said mournfully, "at least throw something that isn't one of a pair."

*Books by Mary McMullen
from Jove*

THE GIFT HORSE
SOMETHING OF THE NIGHT
A GRAVE WITHOUT FLOWERS
UNTIL DEATH DO US PART
THE OTHER SHOE
BETTER OFF DEAD
THE BAD-NEWS MAN
THE DOOM CAMPAIGN
A COUNTRY KIND OF DEATH

A COUNTRY KIND OF DEATH
MARY McMULLEN

JOVE BOOKS, NEW YORK

All of the characters in this book
are fictitious, and any resemblance
to actual persons, living or dead,
is purely coincidental.

This Jove book contains the complete text of the original hardcover
edition. It has been completely reset in a typeface designed for easy
reading and was printed from new film.

A COUNTRY KIND OF DEATH

A Jove Book/published by arrangement with
the author

PRINTING HISTORY
Doubleday & Company edition published 1975
Jove edition/April 1988

ISBN: 0-515-09483-8

Jove Books are published by The Berkley Publishing Group,
200 Madison Avenue, New York, New York 10016.
The name ''JOVE'' and the ''J'' logo
are trademarks belonging to Jove Publications, Inc.

PRINTED IN THE UNITED STATES OF AMERICA

10 9 8 7 6 5 4 3 2 1

ONE

"I think Laddy is going to do something to Mrs. Mint," Kit said.

Donna stuck her bare toe into the water and withdrew it hastily. "Ouch, cold. What do you mean, something?"

"Something bad."

"She's his mother."

"Not his mother. His stepmother."

Kit was seven. Donna was eleven. They were in one of their favorite summertime places, under the broad concrete bridge over Willen's Brook. The banks were soft and grassy and there were big boulders to perch on. Looking out through one arch, you saw a four-foot waterfall sunning and silvering and splashing itself. Through the other arch, you could watch the water curl and froth around its rocks and curve away between willowed banks.

Quivers of light played over the honey-colored concrete above their heads. Donna watched the watery patterns, half hypnotized. She was in a state of mild bliss. School out, and the forever summer before her. So nice to go barefoot, and wear her old blue gingham dress with the torn pocket, and not have to look neat. To pinpoint the morning's perfection, a yellow butterfly hovered four inches above the lip of the waterfall.

She never forgot the yellow butterfly. At moments of great happiness, later in her life, it flickered and bowed in the sunny

1

air, reminding her that no matter how lovely, how secure things looked, there was always . . .

Now she brought herself back to Kit's prophecy. Kit seldom said anything she didn't mean, even if it happened to be a fantasy she firmly believed in at the moment.

"What makes you think that, about Laddy?"

"He watches her, when sometimes she doesn't know he's looking, like—like Dementia flattening down to kill a bird."

"Bird!" Donna giggled. Mrs. Mint was tall and of ample proportions. Lucia said unkindly that she wore her bust at her waist.

"I'll bet it's just this morning that got you thinking this way," she said. "Dr. Munson and all."

Dr. Munson had stopped around to see how their father's bronchitis was clearing up. After pronouncing Philip as hale and well "as a reckless fellow like you will ever get to be" he and Philip shared a leisurely late cup of coffee at the round oak table in the big untidy kitchen.

They were talking about ways of killing people. Philip Keane was a writer of murder stories. His detective was called Inspector Few, of the New York Police Department. Philip often said he wished he could kill *him*, he was so sick of the bastard.

Not in front of the children, Mag always said, absentmindedly and automatically. But Mag, their mother, had left for two months in Europe with their Grandfather Loftus, three days ago.

"Air injected into the vein, by hypodermic," Dr. Munson said enthusiastically. "Absolutely undetectable. Symptoms to the casual medical eye—and believe me there are lots of *those*— would indicate a heart attack. Who'd look for a tiny pinprick?"

"Yes, but that doesn't help me now," Philip said. "My man's gone crashing down a marble stairway. How could the murderer be sure he'd crack his skull open? A concussion is no good to me at all. He'd remember being pushed. Fat in the fire."

They discussed the height and degree of steepness of the stairway, the strength of the push, the angle at which the body was likely to fall.

Kit and Donna half listened, from the living room, where they had been sprawled on the sofa contemplating their morning—Willen's Brook bridge or Mint's Hill?

The conversation they were hearing was as everyday normal to them as the view of the hickories on Mint's Hill through the open top of the Dutch door, the roses scratching at the window screen near the end of the sofa, the ticking of the clock on the mantelpiece over the big stone fireplace.

It wasn't real, the cracked skulls and drowned bodies and mortal wounds with different calibers of bullets, it was just in their father's books. Confined comfortably to sheets of yellow paper with typing on them.

But then, Kit had read Philip's most recent book, in manuscript, and had guessed by page 60 who the murderer was, which at the time had nettled her father considerably. Perhaps there was something in her theory about Laddy and Mrs. Mint, after all.

Donna slipped off her boulder and stretched. "All right, let's go up and take a look around, at Mrs. Mint's. And see if there's anything in the air."

She felt she was too old for it, but sometimes she still played at detecting, with Kit. They would slip out at dusk and sit on the dry stone wall beside the road, under the russet apple tree. Their most relaxing sleuthing called for taking down the license numbers of any cars they considered odd or sinister in appearance, prowling the roadside for spent matches and strangely shaped footprints, and listening intently for the thrilling and terrifying sound of the distant alarm bell which meant that someone had escaped—as happened two or three times every year—from Gordon's Sanatorium, a mile away.

Mrs. Mint's house stood halfway up the long hill that Willen's Road climbed. It had once been a small simple white house, built on two levels to accommodate the slant of the hill, but Mrs. Mint had, with pride and gusto, gotten rid of its simplicity.

There were blue shutters with cutouts in the shape of ducks, blue window boxes full of fiercely red salvia, painted flamingos stuck into the ground on either side of the paved brick path that led from the road to the bright-blue front door with George Washington's head in brass for a knocker.

Mrs. Mint did not allow the Keanes or her stepchildren or any but the most honored visitors to use the front way, as the door opened directly into her living room, a perfect marvel of cleanliness, cretonne, tautly pinned-on antimacassars, rubber plants so dusted and oiled as to seem artificial, china figurines, tapestry-covered footstools, and fat hard upholstered furniture. There were no books, no magazines, newspapers, or ashtrays in the room and it was always kept dark, the cretonne curtains drawn, the shades down, so that the sun couldn't fade its splendors.

A special fascination about Mrs. Mint's house was the grave of her German shepherd, Netty, marked by a concrete slab in the root cellar, a delightfully dim and mysterious place smelling of onions and potatoes and apples and earth. When Mrs. Mint first showed Kit the grave, she had said oracularly, "Out of the storms and rains, the snows and winter winds, there lies Netty, safe in the shelter of her own roof and her own home."

Donna and Kit obediently bypassed the paved walk and turned in at the driveway under heavy dark pines. They found Mrs. Mint in her garden at the back of the house, ferociously pinching off wilted petunia and nasturtium blossoms.

She studied Donna's torn pocket and sniffed.

"I suppose now that it's summer you can be any which way."

Philip said that Mrs. Mint was a termagant and when she wasn't being a termagant she was a virago, and that she had hounded Mr. Mint into his grave.

She was an object of great interest to Donna, with her burning curiosity about everything and everybody and her visible relish in the given moment. Her eyes were a penetrating blue, her cheeks a natural feverish red, her hair dyed a powerful shade of brown, worn in a great loose psyche knot. The gay garden, beautifully kept, seemed a small inadequate stage for her bursting presence.

"Gladys around?" Donna asked, to explain their presence.

"Over to her aunt's this morning." Mrs. Mint sniffed again. "Says she has one of her sick headaches and can't fend for herself. Not Gladys. Rosemary. Too bad the poor thing has none of Mr. Mint's go. Not that he couldn't have used more."

Somehow even her long fleshy nose managed to quiver with contempt when she mentioned her sister-in-law Rosemary.

Then she gave Kit an unexpectedly warm soft smile.

"Hi there, Kit. Glad to be out of school?"

She and Kit had a peculiar, comfortable relationship. They spent considerable time together, talking, as equals. Mrs. Mint, known to keep a tight hand on her larder, lavished Kit with milk, cocoa, tea, cookies, ruthlessly dug for information about what was going on over at the Keanes', and received it freely. In return she told Kit all about her married troubles with Mr. Mint, and all the things that had gone wrong at his grocery store, and how she was feeling, dizzy, or lightheaded, or nauseous, or back-achy, according to the state of her changes.

Kit said innocently, "We wondered if Laddy was around."

"Laddy! You've even forgotten the day of the week now that school's over. Where would he be but at work? Someone's got to keep the place going now that Mr. Mint's passed on."

Mr. Mint had passed on three years ago. Laddy, Lawrence Mint, was nineteen years old. He had gone to work, after high school, at a garage on Cross Street, to learn the business. The owner of the garage had had a large bill outstanding with Mint's Grocery, which Mrs. Mint used as leverage to arrange his apprenticeship.

Laddy had told Donna once that he was going to be an artist and live abroad.

Mrs. Mint's face darkened. "Speaking about Laddy, if you see him with that trashy girl, around town or anywhere, you tell me about it."

Kit knew everything there was to know about the trashy girl. Her name was Edie Avanti, and Laddy fancied himself in love with her. "Grand passion at nineteen! Did you ever hear anything so funny, now, Kit?" Mrs. Mint would give a shout of furious laughter. Edie was no better than she should be. Never mind what that means, Kit, but it's true. Her father drinks at least a gallon of red wine a day. The mother's a dirty housekeeper. They have chickens pecking around their old yard. You should see her wash on the line, Kit, her old bloomers absolutely gray with age—we'll be charitable, won't we?—great rents in her sheets, I drive past there every washday just to get a good laugh. Not what Laddy's used to, Kit, not by any means. You can see the kind of house I keep. And his own sister Gladys, so good, so pretty. I don't believe they even go to church. Not Mint kind of people, the Avantis. I told him in no uncertain terms to stay clear of her. He's a good, quiet boy, Laddy, a bit weak but he's got me to stiffen up his spine, thank God. Have another coconut cookie, do.

Kit often wondered why Laddy Mint just didn't run away. That, she thought, was what she would have done under the circumstances. But there was Edie Avanti, and then, Laddy had loved his father very much.

She had seen him lying in the grass beside Mr. Mint's grave in St. John's Cemetery, half a mile down Willen's Road. It had seemed a little odd to her, but then the old meadowy cemetery was not a frightening place, she and Donna often played there, picked lilies of the valley which apparently no one else wanted, studied the names on the gravestones.

That was one thing she never told Mrs. Mint, about Laddy lying beside his father's grave. As though he wanted his father's company, or thought his father needed Laddy's.

Kit could hardly remember Mr. Mint. A kind, shadowy man with thin hair and rimless glasses, in a white apron, always seeming to be hovering at the back of his grocery store, as though he was retreating from something.

TWO

". . . as far as the girls go, I don't think you'll find them much trouble, they're used to amusing themselves," Mag Keane said in her letter to her sister Therese. "On the whole, I think you'll have a nice peaceful restful summer. Don't mind when Philip gets snarly about his work, he'll recover rapidly, but he's barely approachable before his coffee—which he gets himself, don't bother—and he's pretty well sealed up in his workroom until one o'clock or so, except for tramping in a demented way about the living room or terrace when he's trying to think something out. Attached is a list of days and times for laundry—although they won't pick up if the bill gets over $40—and other such matters, doctor and dentist, etc. Call Philip or write and tell him what train you're taking, there often isn't a cab at the station and it's an almighty distance and expense to the house."

The arrangement had seemed sensible on both sides. Therese had had pneumonia in mid-May and had been advised by her doctor to spend a long leisurely recovery time if she could manage it. Mag had been hesitating about going off to Europe with their father, a retired professor of English, for two long months, but here was the solution.

You magazine (A Monthly of Fashion, Make-up, Hairdos, News, and You) agreed to give Therese a leave of absence. It was with a pleasant sense of being let out of school that she got off the train at the Bedford station on a cloudy gray late morning in June. She didn't know the make of Philip's car and

7

couldn't spot whether it was there or not. The way the Keanes' finances went, feast or famine, it could be a splendid new car or the old one.

The station house was small, its paint peeling. Bedford, in northwestern Connecticut, wasn't in any kind of reasonable commuting distance from New York, which was why the Keanes had fled there from Wilton eight years ago, from too many people and parties and droppers-in and distraction from their work.

"People think that when you work at home you actually don't *work*," Mag said. "They arrive with a bottle or a guest they don't know what to do with and settle down to play with you at any hour of the day or night. It's hell."

In any case, the Keanes did not fit a suburban mold. They were not Girl Scouting, committee-attending, gregarious people. They liked books and solitude and a mildly bohemian, unconforming sort of life.

Therese thought the life would suit her nicely. She was a kind accommodating girl but she had no intention of spending her time cleaning the house and then drinking gin and tonic with five o'clock strangers around a barbecue fire over which the meat usually got charred.

The car, the old one which had picked her up on her last visit two years ago, pulled up to the platform. Philip got out, hugged her, picked up her bags and said, "Happy summer, Therese, glad you could come."

She was immediately and comfortably at home with him.

"I've spoiled a whole morning's work for you. The taxi's sitting over there, after all."

"I was delighted," Philip said, "to be forcibly removed from the bloody typewriter. You remember Kit."

Kit had scrambled from the front seat of the car into the back and was curled into one corner, looking apprehensively at Therese; she already missed her mother, quite badly.

She had shiny soft dark hair cut in bangs, pink cheeks, and large gray-blue eyes with black lashes that Donna said were like awnings. Her face was still round but the dimply body had stretched out a bit and become a thin small one. Therese remembered her as a jolly child, perhaps a little eerily intelligent, direct, trusting, acutely observant.

To Kit, Therese was a figure from the remote past. She hoped she was not going to be like her mother's other sister, Aunt Grace, who was inclined to be brisk and to take a strong interest in how Kit was doing at school and to disapprove of her findings.

Therese felt the delicate, animal wariness and decided to let it dissipate itself without any blandishments on her part. She was not, in any case, an auntly person, she thought. She had no children of her own. Her husband Jonathan had died when his fighter plane went down, three years before. They had been married for two years, almost happy ones, considering that she had been painfully in love with Philip's brother when she had married Jonathan.

She watched Philip's profile and felt the old jolt of the likeness.

He turned his head and smiled at her. "You look nice, Therese, but thinner. I have strict orders from Mag to give you a drink and a light lunch, and send you to bed with a book for the afternoon. If Lucia's rallied round and got your room ready, that is."

Theoretically, the bedroom at the northeast corner of the Keanes' house was the guest room. But Philip used its built-in low shelves to stash away old manuscripts he didn't want confusing him in his workroom. On rainy days, Donna and Kit regarded it as a playroom. And Lucia herself found it a pleasant place to retire to and read, when her own room was too frightfully messed-up and uninhabitable. She had many of her own comforts scattered about, cushions illegally taken from other parts of the house, overdue library books, and plates that reminisced of egg salad sandwiches.

The floors were stained and dusty, the walls needed washing down, the white deep-ruffled organdy curtains were gray. Clutter was everywhere.

This was fine. Lucia could apply herself to serious cleaning only when a room was dramatically dirty and there was a deadline staring her in the face.

She cleaned with speed and strength. She washed and starched the curtains first, and then scrubbed the walls and floors, washed the windows, and dumped all extraneous material, from library books to Philip's manuscripts to Kit's torn Raggedy Ann doll into a huge cardboard carton, which she then carried down to the cellar. She found this easy, as she was a tall, strong girl when she allowed herself to be one. The other Lucia, whom she preferred to be most of the time, was a bit stooped because of her annoying height, and dreamily disorganized.

She had ironed the curtains and hung them and was whipping fresh sheets over the bed when she found the hat.

Cap, rather. A navy-blue knitted cap, wintry-looking. She recognized it as Laddy Mint's. Someone had stuffed it between the mattress and the boxspring. Mildly puzzled, she looked at it. As a Keane, she was not surprised to find articles in places where you did not expect them to be, but still, Laddy's cap?

From her mountaintop of sixteen years, Lucia thought, good heavens, is one of them going through that boring stealing period? Kit, maybe?

Donna, acting on orders, came in with a pewter pitcher filled with field daisies she had picked, and black-eyed Susans, and the pink wild geraniums she knew would fade and die in an hour or so but which she never could resist gathering.

"Why Laddy's hat?" Lucia asked.

"I don't know. I'll ask Kit. The room looks nice, Lucia. There's the car."

"That's just how I figured it," Lucia said triumphantly.

Therese entered the house as a quiet presence. There was no fuss or inordinate kissing and crying out of joyful greetings. No demand that shoes be put on and baths be taken and meals eaten at regular hours. No gimlet-eyed inspection of clothing or clucking over the sight of Dementia the cat sleeping on the kitchen counter. All of which could have been expected upon Aunt Grace's arrival.

By two o'clock, she was in bed with her book, enjoying the crispness of the sheets, smelling with faint amusement the powerful odors of bleach and soap powder from still-damp walls, floors, and woodwork, and listened to the sounds that were to replace for a while her New York noises. Hickory leaves rustling in the breeze, against the screen. A sudden infuriated screech from the parrot Peg, sitting on her perch in

Philip's workroom. A car climbing Willen's Road. Donna's voice floating up from the great long stone terrace, its walls buried in pink and red rambler roses, that ran the length of the house front . . .

"Kit, if you've lost the hoe again I'll murder you dead."

"It's not *the* hoe, it's my hoe, for Christmas." Kit's voice, clear and sweet.

From deep in Therese's memory came a picture of that cherished present in the depths of winter, the tied-together small rake, hoe, and shovel, with brightly painted red or blue handles. You tried out your rake on the caked cold leaves, your shovel on the harsh unyielding earth, and thought of May, and flowers. And then when the spring came around, somehow you could never remember where you had put those beloved tools.

Donna, who had planned to work in her garden for a while, exhausted her energy finding the hoe. It turned up deep in the ramblers, under the terrace wall.

"Kit . . ." the voice seeming to come from far away as Therese's eyelids grew heavy. "Lucia found Laddy's cap in the guest room, hidden. Did you put it there?"

"Yes. I didn't steal it, I found it."

"Why save a dirty old cap?"

"That's for the scent," Kit said, "if we ever need a bloodhound to find Laddy."

"Oh, Kit . . . you fool."

Laddy? Bloodhounds, on an afternoon that smelled of roses and murmured with leaves.

Therese was half-smiling when she fell asleep.

THREE

"Best time of the day," Philip Keane said, vigorously stirring martinis in a battered ivory-colored crock which had once held ginger beer from Scotland.

Seeing Therese's interested gray eyes on the crock, he explained. "Angus MacPherson—you remember Angus, the distinguished, mad Scot—brings this to me so he can have a proper shandygaff when he demands it. He says he won't drink any of my American muck. He's only been in this country twenty years."

Therese very vividly remembered Angus because at a party at the Keanes he had gotten angry with something his wife Fay said and had thrown a plate of crackers and cheese at her. She had retaliated with a bucket of ice cubes. Neither had sustained serious injuries in this encounter.

Angus, she knew, was an eminent writer of novels of the sea. His name was spoken gravely in English literature classes; he had a Pulitzer Prize under his belt. His temper was legendary. The MacPhersons were old and close friends of the Keanes; Fay, she seemed to recall, was Angus's third wife.

Philip handed her her drink and sat down in his wing chair. Dutifully, before her first cold sip, Therese asked, "Where are the children? Everything all right?"

"Life went on while you slept," Philip said with a grin. "They're around somewhere. They turn up, like dogs, at dinnertime."

Late sunlight suddenly spotlit him in his chair. He got up with an annoyed nervous movement and yanked down a shade that had a tear in it. He looked tired and pale—working hard, she supposed—and his brown-gray hair was tousled. He was a thin wiry man in his early forties, with strong rough elegant bones—like Patrick's, she thought, only everything about Patrick was a bit bigger. Philip's eyes were a clear intelligent hazel, Patrick's were—and then, she couldn't remember. Probably hazel too.

"The book?" she asked tentatively.

"Don't mention it, we're supposed to be enjoying ourselves," Philip said. "I've painted myself into a corner. I'll paint myself out of it somehow. Let joy be unconfined, Therese. No cooking for you tonight, Lucia's going to rattle something together."

They talked amiably about what she'd been doing on *You* magazine, and about the state of the world, which Philip found hopeless; and where Mag would be right now, and what she and her father would be doing.

"Yoohoo," a voice called, in high, half-singing syllables. The Dutch door was all the way open and showed Mrs. Mint approaching across the terrace. She gave a purely formal light knock on the wooden bar of the screen door and entered with bright confidence. Donna slipped in behind her and went to sit in a far corner of the room.

Mrs. Mint was carrying a bowl of plums.

"Evening, Philip, evening, Mrs. Vane, you remember me? . . . Just a little nice fresh fruit for you, Mag told me you'd been ill, there's nothing like our Bedford air to clear that up."

Kit appeared from nowhere and sat down on the step between the living room and the dining room.

Donna admired the bold style of Mrs. Mint's entry, seeing that she was a little afraid of Philip. But of course, she would want to take an early look at Therese. Philip always fled when she came over to gossip with Mag, muttering about his work. "That *is* the hardest-working man in town," Mrs. Mint would cry enthusiastically. "I've never seen him sit down once, all the times I've been there. And they say writers have easy lives!"

Without waiting for an invitation, Mrs. Mint flopped on the

sofa beside Therese and got a handkerchief from her pocket and mopped her face.

"Don't let me interrupt anything," she said. "My knees are a bit shaky. I've suddenly come a little dizzy all over."

Her changes, Kit thought sympathetically.

Philip, who was determindedly selfish about his cocktail time, just manged to erase a scowl and said, "I suppose you won't have a drink? . . . Donna, get Mrs. Mint a cup of tea or something. We'll take our drinks out on the terrace and let you rest quietly in here."

Therese was taken aback by his rudeness but imagined in his kind of life it must be a brutal necessity.

"No, no—no tea—I only need a minute to catch my breath and I'll be off," Mrs. Mint said, bridling. "I'm sure I don't like to be in the way. It's just that I had a near-fall and I'm a bit shaky—"

There was to be no escaping the story of her near-fall. Philip downed his drink and got another one.

It was that delivery boy from Mint's, Mrs. Mint said, explaining in an aside to Therese that they still dealt with Mint's Grocery even though it had been sold to Higgins shortly after Mr. Mint's death—"and precious little it brought, highway robbery I'd call it."

The boy was lazy and slow and always late with deliveries. She'd spoken a word to Higgins about him and given the boy a good taste of her tongue in front of some of the other customers. Well, this afternoon, he'd been late as usual, and he hadn't even carried up her order but left it at the bottom of the garage stairs, God only knew how long it had been sitting there spoiling, and flies all around no doubt . . . She noticed one of the sticks of butter had been crushed in transit, the waxy paper split open, the butter all dented, and at the price of butter . . .

When she left the house, she usually used the inside back stairway from the kitchen to the garage. Just now, she had been going down the stairs when suddenly, six steps from the bottom, she had slipped and fallen heavily on her . . .

"Ass," Philip said helpfully, over her pause.

"My coccyx." Mrs. Mint sniffed. "Even when my knees are

bad I'm surefooted. I must be up and down those stairs a dozen times a day. Well, I studied that stair where I slipped and do you know what it was smeared with? Butter!''

Kit's eyes met Donna's in a long slow look.

"Butter," Philip said thoughtfully, "on the marble step, quite high up . . . but they'd see it on the soles of his shoes."

Donna said, "They could have taken his shoes off and burned or hid them or threw them in a pond."

Kit added, "And wiped away the butter, with a cloth, so nobody would ever know how he slipped."

Mrs. Mint stared.

Kit abruptly abandoned the problems of her father's plot and addressed herself to Mrs. Mint, in an offhand kindly way.

"Was there anyone there to pick you up, Mrs. Mint? Laddy—"

"Certainly not, miss, I picked myself up. Laddy was at work of course, he has a family to support. I'll have the truth out of that boy of Higgins's, you'll see if I don't."

"Laddy has it rough," Philip said. "How old is he—nineteen? And do you still do substitute teaching, Mrs. Mint?"

She got his message and flushed.

"I'm a martyr to my dizzy spells," she said, pointedly addressing Therese. "Things go black." She looked, recovering now, robust, throbbing with life, a martyr to nothing or nobody.

The screen door opened again, this time with a violent jerk. Fay MacPherson rushed in. She was clutching a battered manila folder.

"Quick!" she cried. "Lock every door. Lock every window. Angus is after me and we haven't got more than five minutes at best—"

"Drink time in the old corral," Philip muttered grimly to Therese. "Girls, up and at it."

Mrs. Mint settled deeper into the sofa and said delightedly, "I must go, that is, as soon as my knees will hold me up—"

Fay, panting, seized Philip's ginger beer crock and poured its contents into a glass. She was a tall handsome woman in her thirties, richly hipped and breasted. She had a flaring high color, a thick mane of dark hair and protuberant dark eyes.

"What seems to be the trouble now?" Philip asked, to the

accompaniment of windows being slammed down and latched. He got up and closed and bolted the front door.

Fay, who was having trouble trying to smoke and drink simultaneously, said, "It's my book. I've been hiding pages away and he found and tried to destroy a whole chapter. Fortunately I managed to snatch it back from him. He flew into an absolutely maniacal rage and came after me with the poker. I was near the window but I had to jump into the middle of the rosebushes. My car's hidden in Mindon Lane. I ran all the way here."

Her legs, indeed, were scratched and bleeding and her hair wild.

"Fay," Philip explained to Therese, "is writing a biography of her husband. It's called—what was your most recent title, Fay, *The Murky Sea?*"

"History should see him whole," Fay cried. "The bad with the good. The devils in him along with the angels. I feel it a duty."

She brandished her folder. "As a matter of fact, I brought the manuscript here with me to hide. I'll bring over other chapters as I finish them."

"You don't suppose," Philip said, "that Agnus might fly into another rage and burn the house down to destroy your biography?"

Fay considered this for a moment, sipping and relishing her martini.

"No . . . certainly not if he thought there was anyone *in* the house. I won't tell you where I'm going to hide it, so you won't have the responsibility if he comes in here with a rifle or something."

The room went very dim as she pulled down the shade of the other window fronting the terrace.

"After the front door, he'll try the back, of course," she said to Philip. "Answer him at the back without opening up. Tell him I telephoned you to say I was going to stay with my mother in New York. I'll sleep in Mag's studio tonight and by tomorrow he should be all right."

There was a tremendous banging and thundering at the door. Not polite knuckles; a fist crashing.

"Let me in!" a voice roared. "Let me get at that wench!"

Fay finished her drink and mixed another. "I don't dare rattle any ice cubes," she whispered. "I'll just have it straight . . . back door in just a minute, I think, Philip."

Therese found herself a little frightened by the violence, the feeling of being in a house under siege. She put out a hand—looking for comfort, bestowing it?—to Donna, sitting very upright on a footstool near her.

Donna had always struck her as a brave, adventurous child. She was thin and taut, with hair the color of an old penny, blue-white skin, and freckles that looked green, and larger, when she was tired or frightened. They looked large now. She had a wry thin clever face, and a kind of airy independence. She knew Lucia was her father's favorite and thought Kit was her mother's, and had decided early that, all right, she would go it sort of alone.

She responded with a shy attractive three-cornered smile to Therese's touch. Her eyes were a color between green and blue.

"It's okay," she murmured. "Dad will get rid of him. There he is at the back now."

Yes, Mag, fine, Mag, Therese thought.

". . . on the whole, I think you'll have a nice peaceful restful summer."

FOUR

What seemed to be peace had fallen, at least temporarily, upon the Keane household.

Last night had continued hectic. Lucia, reading while she cooked, burned the spaghetti.

Fay, to whom several strong martinis had given a sharp appetite, was the first to pronounce the spaghetti inedible. She went into the kitchen and used up almost the whole week's eggs and all the cheese and made a magnificent soufflé.

Angus, handled at the back door by Philip, had gulped the restoring scotch and water that Philip gave him, made a loud snorting noise when told Fay had gone to her mother's in New York, and stamped off down the back steps.

"That wench," he said over his shoulder to Philip, "will jump out of one of my windows once too often."

Later, there was a commotion about bedclothes for Fay to take out to the studio. There were, it turned out, no clean sheets. Lucia found an old quilted cotton comforter which, Fay said, smelled of Dementia but she supposed it was better than nothing.

Fay and Philip stayed up late, talking and drinking beer. Therese, suddenly blank with exhaustion, left them to it a little after eleven and slept and dreamed of Patrick Keane.

She came down in the morning to find Donna in the kitchen, drinking orange juice, and Fay making herself a sumptuous breakfast of the last two of the eggs, poached in mushroom soup, with marmalade on toasted English muffins to follow.

Therese usually breakfasted on a soft-boiled egg. She made do without it and poured a cup of coffee. Donna studied her shyly, curiously. The white silk shirt with the sleeves rolled up, the white linen shorts, beautifully tailored, with stitched silk arrows at the pocket corners. The white thong sandals.

In an affable way, *You* magazine had sent Therese to Bermuda a few weeks after she got out of the hospital to supervise a fashion feature on one of their new colors, Bermuda Sand. In the course of her stay there, Therese had acquired an apricot-golden color on her legs and arms and face.

She was small and slender, with brown shining hair cut just short of her shoulders, and side-parted. Her face was quiet but with its subtle changes of expression reminded Donna of the rippling reflections under the concrete bridge. There was no particular competition from any other feature to distract from the mysterious beauty of soft gray eyes, eyes as full of light and depth as rain and cloud with the sun trying to break through.

Donna thought that, in the middle of the disaster the Keanes' kitchen became every morning, she looked like a strange white and brown bird, and very wonderful.

Fay monopolized the bathroom for an hour, used up all the hot water in her bath, and drove home to Angus.

"What will happen?" Therese asked Donna.

"Nothing, I think. He'll have broken some of their china, though. He works from early in the morning until after three. By that time he'll probably have forgotten all about yesterday. Fay will have his tea waiting for him, when he stops working. She puts two shots of scotch into it. Then he takes a five-mile walk—like Dad—alone."

"And all will be quiet until the next time?"

"Yes," Donna said.

With a recollection of the mention of Angus's rifle, Therese asked, "Do you know where she hid the manuscript? Or her chapters, or whatever?"

"Somewhere in the studio, I should think. She carried the folder out there with her quilt."

Mag's studio was beyond the back apple orchard, near the grape arbor and the old well and a jungle of blackberry bushes.

Well, at least, a safe distance from the house, if Angus did resort to incendiary measures.

It was Donna's week for the kitchen. She tackled without complaint what looked like the remains of several dozens of breakfasts.

Now—a little guiltily savoring the silence, she would make up for it later by washing some of the girls' dirty clothes— Therese sat in a lawn chair under an apple tree, a book in her lap, contemplating the perfections of the morning.

The lawn rose and fell over its hill, which peaked at the terrace steps. This was a country of steeps and rises and hills. Facing her, to her left, was Mrs. Mint's house, beyond a long grassy dip, sitting on its own hill among pines and hickories. To her right, the great shoulder of Mint's Hill, at its feet a daisied meadow which dipped here and there into frog-singing swamps. The Keane property, roughly three acres, and the Mints' land, perhaps four acres, formed a sort of square, bounded on two sides by the sharply curving Willen's Brook, and on the other two sides by Willen's Road and Mindon Lane.

Fortunately for their often precarious financial state, the Keanes owned their pleasantly rambling white clapboarded house and their three acres. Philip Keane's one and only rich relative, an Uncle Sergius, had died and left him money and he put it into the house, which they had been renting.

It was, Therese supposed, an isolated life for the Keane girls, this far away from town and other neighbors, but as Mag had said they appeared to be perfectly happy amusing themselves. Donna and Kit seemed to have only one friend, or companion, nearby, Gladys Mint, thirteen years old. Lucia took her social life more seriously and often bicycled off into Bedford, always, on command from Philip, leaving a note by the telephone saying where she was and at what number she could be reached.

A clatter of pots from the kitchen—every pot and pan in the house seemed to have been used this morning. An almost inaudible mumble and drone of insects in the grass. An oriole dripping sweet notes like sparkles of water, falling. Sunlight and shadow, dappling, floating, over her open book.

The shadow solidified. The dapples disappeared. Startled, she looked up. He had made no sound approaching but of course the grass would still his footsteps.

"Hello," the boy said. "You'd be Mrs. Vane?"

She vaguely remembered seeing him, once or twice, years ago. He was slim, a little over medium height, with crimpy-curly light brown hair, very pale blue eyes with a fixed expression, a straight nose, and a small straight mouth with very little lip. His mild good looks seemed superficial, without bone or style to back them up. She got an impression of some weakness—physical?—his back should have been straighter, his shoulders harder and squarer. Or emotional? Perhaps it was living with Mrs. Mint. He hardly looked a match for that lusty presence; there must be something draining about it, Mrs. Mint's blazing vitality sucking up her stepson's lesser portion of it like a blotter.

His voice was polite and a little higher than one would have expected. Laddy has it rough, Philip had said. He didn't look unhappy. Secretive, perhaps, and bland. Some sort of shield . . .

Therese said yes, she was Mrs. Vane.

"I'm sorry to bother you but it was my mother's idea. I work at Elder's Garage and they have cars for hire. She thought you might like a car while you're here . . ." he trailed off, as if he felt it a very unlikely wish on her part.

"That's very kind of Mrs. Mint," Therese said briskly. "I don't at the moment but if the need arises I'll remember your garage. Are they expensive?"

"Not too bad." His face brightened. "There's a blue convertible, a Buick, she's a nice car. I've just finished her new transmission and she's in perfect shape."

"Good. I'll remember to ask for the blue Buick."

He lingered, seeming not to know how to shape an exit line.

"*Lad-dee!*" A carrying shriek from Mrs. Mint, standing in her garden, waving her arms like a windmill. "Don't be dithering around Mrs. Vane. Just tell her about the cars and let her be."

"Oh, well, then . . ." He blushed in uncomfortable patches. "Elder's, the name is. Goodbye, Mrs. Vane."

She watched him go down the long-grassed slope, head hanging a little. Why wasn't he at work? Oh yes, today was Saturday.

The old, summer timelessness had begun. She started to read, and out of the corner of her eye saw Kit following close after Laddy. Such a little girl, and such a . . . in ways, strange boy. Thrust the stupid shadow of a worry aside. This wasn't some bucolic corner of Hardyesque England, this was Bedford, Connecticut, on a day in June, and Laddy Mint was the boy next door.

Kit thought it wouldn't hurt if she kept an eye on Laddy, every now and then. She didn't think it would seem peculiar to him. She was a constant visitor at Mrs. Mint's.

From behind the willows, she heard the quarrel.

In the long hollow between Mrs. Mint's house hill and big Mint's Hill was a pond, known officially as Mrs. Mint's fishpond. In it she kept her family of goldfish, winter and summer. There were at least three dozen of them, grown very large, some measuring seven and eight inches long.

Mrs. Mint would kneel on the grassy bank over the water, reach down and ruffle the surface with a stick she kept handy, and call her goldfish. "Come, little fishies. Come to mother."

And they would come, flashing rose and red and orange and silver-gold, while she flung their fish food to them.

The pond was large, about 70 feet long, deep enough for swimming, deep enough to dive into from the grassy feeding station, even, but Mrs. Mint did not and could not swim and the girls only used it in extremes of heat, as the bottom was slippery with weeds and the water felt overwarm and viscous. Besides, you hardly liked fish swimming around you; Kit had a theory that they might bite.

The thick young willows stood close to the near end of the pond.

"You've been seeing that nasty little bitch," Mrs. Mint said, quite near Kit.

"Have not."

"Someone, never mind who, saw you with her and told me. Going into the movies, you were, last night."

"For Christ's sake, if you're going to have the whole town spying on me—"

"Don't you dare swear and curse at me, Laddy Mint," Mrs.

Mint shrieked, "or nineteen or not I'll wash your mouth out with soap. Trash, trash, no better than a whore, as maybe by now you've found out—"

There was a scuffling sound and a scream from Mrs. Mint.

"Keep your hands off me!" A tremendous, resounding slap, no question of who delivered it to whom. Mrs. Mint was panting. "—to raise a hand against your own mother, that'll show you—"

"Stepmother."

"—who's cared for you in sickness and in health, and fed and clothed you and worried over you morning, noon, and night, and now not even a man in the house to turn to—"

"I'm a man." He sounded breathless.

"*You!*" Mrs. Mint laughed loudly. "Green love-sick kid running after a little wop after all the others are finished with her—"

"I'll kill you if you don't leave off Edie." His voice rising, now.

"It's the other way around, young fellow. Quite the other way around. Now off with you, at least I don't have to put up with that boy of Higgins's today. The grocery list's on the kitchen table. You can take my car. And don't go around by way of the Avantis."

Kit did not immediately reveal her presence; she thought it might not be tactful. Quarrels seemed to hover in the very air about Mrs. Mint's head, but Kit had found this one a little out of the ordinary, a little frightening. Mrs. Mint didn't usually use such bad words; but then, she hadn't known Kit was there and had no reason to temper her language.

In any case, Mrs. Mint would be quite safe for a while, if Laddy was off after the groceries.

She would need a little time to recover herself. People did, after quarrels. Kit beat a silent retreat and went up the slope to her own lawn.

If someone was going to kill someone, they wouldn't come right out and tell the person about it. Would they?

Donna had said yesterday that she'd murder her if she had lost her own hoe.

Nevertheless, with a vague recollection of a scene in one of her father's books, she found a pencil and a piece of paper, and carefully wrote down the quarrelsome exchange between Laddy and Mrs. Mint; she had a highly retentive memory. She had learned to write before she went to school, and there they had taught her a form of printing; her hand was an odd mixture of both, but to her perfectly readable.

She considered for a moment, and then decided on her garden as a hiding place.

Each of them had a garden. Lucia's was out near her mother's studio but had been abruptly abandoned last year. Donna's was at the side of the house, under a mulberry tree. Kit's was a considerable distance away, down by the front gate on Willen's Road, which wasn't a gate at all but an opening in the dry stone wall.

Her garden measured about 6 by 8 feet and was in a sorry state. Dusty miniature marigolds and a few lavender cosmos struggled with wild mustard and Queen Anne's lace. There were a good many bare patches where seeds put in so hopefully hadn't come up at all, but then Donna told her at the time she was planting them too early and the late frost would get them. The whole arrangement was badly in need of water. Around the garden, to hem it, Kit had laboriously placed the large stones Philip had unearthed in the process of digging it up for her.

She lifted one of the larger stones, looked with distaste at the withered white-green grass under it, and two white sluglike things, squirming, but the grass felt dry to her dirty palm. She put the note down and replaced the stone.

Therese, cleaning the bathroom, looked out the window and saw the small squatting shape, the sun on the shiny hair.

Dear little thing, she thought. Working in her garden. Funny little Kit.

No one noticed Kit in the act of hiding her piece of paper except an attentive robin in a nearby russet apple tree, and Gladys Mint, from the window of her pink and white bedroom.

FIVE

Philip, struggling with a scene in Chapter 11, cursed beer and Angus and especially Fay, who, as he put it to himself, had kept him up until two o'clock in the morning.

He left his silently scolding typewriter and went out of his workroom through the living room to the terrace, where hard striding might make his brain start ticking over.

His irate eye caught Lucia, sprawled on her back on the broad terrace wall, under the branches of the hickory tree. There was a 12-foot drop on the other side of the wall.

Talk about the peace and quiet of the country, Philip often would say. Trees to fall out of. Wells to fall into. Copperheads in the woods. Ice to crack and drown the skater. Wasps that—if they got you in the right place—could kill you. Ropes on swings to fray and snap when the swinger was soaring high in the air. Cars going by at murderous speeds to destroy the careless bicyclist.

"What the hell are you doing, lounging about on the edge of a precipice?" he asked angrily. "Get up at once. To say nothing of wasting a perfect beautiful summer morning—"

Lucia preserved her dignity by sitting up in a very leisurely way before she slid her legs to the terrace floor. She had Philip's hazel eyes, beautiful fair skin, thick and moist and mat-finished, and long soft hair between brown and blond, a wet sand color. In spite of his irritation, Philip softened at the gangly boneless gracefulness of her.

Something about the sweet sensuous curve of her mouth, her air of sleepy expectancy, squeezed at him painfully.

Perhaps it hadn't been a good thing, Mag going away the summer when Lucia was being sixteen.

Therese was a nice young woman, but obviously with no experience of the things innocent-looking kids could be actually up to . . .

"I'm going somewhere soon," Lucia explained vaguely. "I was just waiting for it to be time."

"Waiting and wasting are two different things," Philip said severely. "I'd suggest you improve the shining hour by going out to your mother's studio and tidying it. Fay probably left it in a shambles."

This suggestion suited Lucia perfectly, as she had planned to melt quietly away to the studio, soon. Now she was being ordered to go there.

"I'll just get some things from the house. Cleaning things."

Cleaning things . . . Suppose someone had left a full pail of soapy water on the marble staircase down which his man was pitched. Then, if he hadn't been killed on impact, the pail could be swung with a tremendous whack against his head. It would be assumed that it had come thundering down after him and struck him . . . worth a try, anyway. Philip went back to his workroom.

Lucia wrote on the pad by the telephone, *Bensons*. Jane Benson, by prearrangement, would cover for her. She took a broom and her bathing suit and a towel, wrapped up in an old dustcloth, out to the studio.

It had once been a playhouse built for forgotten children. It was a small one-room structure of weathered unpainted shingles with a green roof and green shutters. The air inside was green, too, from the drooping branches of the apple tree near the door.

Mag was, in a small way, a sculptor. She sold occasional garden pieces, nymphs and fauns and cherubs, to Holden's Nursery. She did, on commission, busts of Bedford's better-heeled young children. Her biggest coup had been a bust of Nathaniel Warren, president of the Bedford Bank and Trust Company.

There were blocks of stone and marble about, cans of sand

and heavy iron trays, tools and implements hung on nails. There was a hotplate on a peeling wooden table, and at the far end a folding bed, draped now with the rumpled quilt. An overflowing ashtray on the floor beside it, an empty beer bottle with flies buzzing at its neck, a plate with cracker crumbs and a rind of cheese and an apple core on it. Fay must have carried a late snack to bed with her. She had forgotten her pink slip; it was hooked over the single straight-backed wooden chair the room held.

"Pig," Lucia said indignantly. She made short work of tidying up. The round old Big Ben ticked loudly in the silence. That nice boy—well, man, really, twenty-two, Joe Something—was going to pick her up here at eleven. He was a house guest of the Powells. Philip didn't like or approve of the Powells and had told her he didn't want her seeing them.

Fortunately, you couldn't see the studio from the house. They were going to go swimming in Mindon Lake, two miles away.

There was no place to change there, so Lucia stripped and put on her bathing suit and then put her sundress back on over it. She was just buttoning the shoulder of the dress when she saw the round face peering in at the open screened window.

"Nasty little spy," Lucia hissed. She was feeling guilty. She loved her father, but still. A swim on a summer morning with people all around—and he hadn't even met Joe, so he could hardly disapprove of him.

Gladys Mint came around to the open door of the studio. She was a pink, plump girl with very dark hair and eyes and a mild gentle manner. Her specialty was being good. Always clean, polite, dutiful, wanting to run errands for people. Lucia considered her another of the boring pack of kids who surrounded her, and a snoop into the bargain.

Gladys giggled. "I saw you put on your bathing suit. You didn't know I was there for the longest time. I was practicing not breathing. Are you going to jump into the well and take a swim?"

"Someone will be in the well if they don't shut up," Lucia said.

Gladys's eyes widened; now she sensed a secret.

"Are Donna and Kit coming with you? To swim? Can I come? Mother will let me, I know, if your aunt is taking you to the lake."

"No one's going swimming. I'm going to take a sunbath. And this," Lucia said, lapsing back a few years, "is private property. Beat it."

The Keanes had no servants but, from her reading, Lucia thought that Gladys looked like an offended parlormaid.

"I know where I'm not wanted," she said. "Don't worry. I hope you enjoy your—*sunbath.*"

Little sneak, Lucia thought. She'll probably tell someone. But then, her father never listened to anything any of the Mints said.

To occupy the fifteen minutes before Joe was due, she hunted for Fay's folder. She found it under an almost completed life-size head of Kit in rough stipply plaster; a dirty green cloth lay around the neck and shoulder, concealing the edge of the folder.

Without a great deal of interest, she flipped it open.

". . . Angus's first and second wives were in effect a rehearsal for me. He finds in me Elena's fire, her passion (but, in my case, in a *raffinée* way, Elena was a Pole, the daughter of a coal miner); and Barbara's incisive analytical brain, so helpful when he comes to a problem in his work. In his droll Scots way, he often says, 'A mind and a boody, what muir cod a mon want?' "

Lucia grinned. Dreadfully rendered dialect, and she could not imagine Angus ever saying such a thing to Fay, or being described under any circumstances as droll.

A conspiratorial male voice outside the screen door. "Lukie?" He had already coined his own nickname for her. It delighted her.

"Sssshhh. Rats and sneaks and kids about. Coming, Joe."

SIX

"I ought to warn you," Donna said to Therese, "people usually descend on this place on Saturday nights."

"People? What people?" Therese asked in mild alarm. They were sitting on the terrace steps, peacefully shelling peas. Kit was within view, sitting beside the birdbath in Mrs. Mint's garden while Mrs. Mint weeded.

"Their friends," Donna said. "They aren't asked especially, they just come. It isn't planned, there's no food to lay out or anything, they just get what they want when they're hungry and often they bring bottles."

"They" began in Therese's mind to swell into formidable numbers; she almost heard the sound of distant feet marching on the Keanes'.

"When do they come?"

"Oh, not until after dinner sometime, don't worry."

Therese's very good fried chicken and peas and mashed potatoes had been consumed and Donna had finished cleaning up the kitchen when the first guest drifted in.

Therese was in her bedroom, changing from her shirt and shorts into a bare-shouldered black pique dress and black sandals when she heard the shout.

"Greetings, you old bastard!"

This turned out to be the eminent songwriter Johnny Coe. He was joined in rapid succession by Angus and Fay, temporarily in harmony; one of Therese's favorite cartoonists, Van

31

Moore, looking, predictably, the picture of gloom; a man from *The New York Times,* who immediately fell into a ferocious argument with Angus about politics; an elegant Franciscan monk from the monastery outside Bedford, near Brookfield Center; Elaine Bunter, the novelist, who showed an ill-concealed passion for Moore any and every time her husband left the room to get another drink; and, mysteriously, the local undertaker, a man named Sable.

In the course of the evening, it emerged that Mr. Sable dabbled in land on the side and had dropped by to see if Philip would be interested in picking up an acre on the other side of Willen's Brook to "finish off your estate."

"Coming from you, I don't quite like those words," Philip said, which was only one of the merciless remarks the long-suffering Sable had to endure that night. He showed, however, no inclination to leave.

The party flowed from room to room and out onto the terrace. Johnny Coe played the piano, an old upright relegated to Philip's workroom as nobody any longer had any interest in it. It was a new song he was working on and he played bits and pieces of it over and over. It was to be called, "All for the Love of You."

The sound of the piano enraged the parrot Peg, sitting on her perch driven into the stone chimney breast above the work-room fireplace. She stalked up and down the perch sideways, her eyes flaring red, and repeatedly screamed the only words she had ever produced, *"Por Dios!"*

She had been a present from Angus, brought back from Guatemala, and had been accepted without a great deal of enthusiasm by the senior Keanes. The children spent one fascinated week trying to teach her to talk and sing, learned to keep well out of reach of her beak, and then dropped her cold. Philip had a sort of cranky fondness for her and she for him. Several times each summer she escaped, usually alighting high in a hickory tree on Mint's Hill, and there was a tremendous fuss and outcry and ladder-maneuvering before she was brought back safely.

Donna stayed up until well after eleven, when Philip spotted her, sitting on the dining-room stairs hugging her bony knees, and said, Bed.

She retreated six stairs higher up, into the shadows, not wanting to lose the thread of two conversations she was listening to simultaneously, Van Moore demanding from Mr. Sable details of the funniest funeral he had ever undertaken, and Elaine Bunter talking to the elegant Franciscan about sex.

Lucia stole a scotch and water that was sitting untouched on the kitchen table, not because she liked it but because she refused to be classed with the children. Stretched out on her bed with a book, she didn't read but thought about Joe, whose last name emerged as Bolt. There had been a lot of people at the lake, but under the stingingly cold water, way under, he had peeled her bathing suit down to her waist. Wanting air, she had shot quite soon to the surface, and he had said, laughing and spitting water, "Oh, you country girls. Don't you ever get around?"

She wasn't sure she liked this feeling of being on an express train, going somewhere very fast, she didn't know where.

"Oh, the precious little *thing!*" Elaine Bunter cried, to show her motherly side to Van Moore. He was not impressed; he hated children.

Kit came walking slowly, but sure-footed and graceful, down the stairway. Her pink pajamas were the color of her cheeks. Her eyes were wide and shining.

Philip put a finger to his lips and followed a little behind her. She went to the chair her mother usually sat in and thoughtfully touched its arm. She stood quite still, then turned and purposefully mounted the stairs again.

"Asleep?" the monk asked, interested.

"Yes . . . she misses her mother . . ." He took a quick look, upstairs. Donna could be heard scrubbing her teeth in the bathroom. Kit was back in bed, deeply asleep.

Therese was quite happy leaning against the piano and watching Johnny Coe's flying fingers. He flirted extravagantly with her, singing the words of his song at her, to her; she joined in, her voice light, gay and true.

He did, for her, a run-through of his hit songs. "Oh-oh Oriole," "Don't Dress, Put on Any Old Thing for Me," "Heavens Above, Love," "Moon after Moon," "By Golly,

That Grand Old Trolley,'' and, to season the sweet corn of his "Trolley," the lovely haunting "Pray Forget Me." *The New York Times*man spotted her there, singing, in her slender black dress, and came over to her and began to breathe heavily.

Kit woke some time in the night to hear voices directly under the casement windows of the room she shared with Donna.

"... an enchanting book ..." Fay's voice, even thicker and plummier than in the daytime.

"Oh, well, *thank* you." Mrs. Bunter. High thin sound. She was English.

"Not your book. My book."

"Indeed. I didn't know you wrote. Have you got a publisher?"

"I wouldn't, or I don't think I would, like to have Angus's people do it, there would be something incestuous about that, perhaps Philip's publisher, Coxwain ... there may be quite a rush for it."

"No doubt. A new book by an unknown. No doubt ..."

The voices drifted away. Kit, wide awake, knelt on her bed and looked out of the window. No lights in Mrs. Mint's house, but lights from the Keane house paled the terrace, the tumbling roses and the round mounded lawn.

She felt the need of motion, but didn't want to go downstairs, where people would rumple her hair and tell her how sweet she was, until her father spotted her and ordered her back to bed. There was a lot of noise, music from the radio, talking, laughter, shouting from Angus. It might, she knew, go on until it got light.

She said to the sleeping shape in the bed at right angles to hers, "Donna?"

Donna always slept like a stone. She didn't wake.

Kit crept through the open casement window onto the slanting shingled eaves, turned cautiously around, got a good grip on the copper drainpipe along the edge of the eaves, and let her small light body drop over. It was three feet down to the terrace. There was a familiar shock as her soles hit the rough stones.

The stones were warm and the night was soft, with a faint breeze. There was a round bright moon hanging what seemed to be several inches above Mint's Hill, as though it would entangle itself in the hickory branches.

She thought about Mrs. Mint and how, when you were asleep, anybody could do anything to you. She herself always checked carefully for lions under the bed before getting in between the sheets, harking back to a wholly forgotten incident of an escaped lion, from a little traveling circus that had pitched its tents in the meadow beyond Willen's Brook.

Mrs. Mint, Gladys had told her, took her teeth out when she went to bed and put them in a glass of water on the bedside table. Mrs. Mint, toothless, seemed even more vulnerable and helpless as she lay asleep.

Kit went swiftly down the terrace steps, across the top of the lawn and down the slope. As she approached the willows, where her path would turn left to climb Mrs. Mint's hill, she heard a chuckling watery sound.

She moved softly into the willows and peered through the floating tangly strands. The moon made a long white oval of the pond, with something round and black on the surface at the end of it, very near her. Laddy. Laddy, just standing in the pool with his head sticking out, or perhaps treading water. If he was swimming, his feet and arms would show too, there would be kicking and foam.

He moved again, to the same unearthly chuckle of water in the night. All but the top of his head disappeared.

Why wasn't he swimming? He could, she knew. It was as if he was just making sure how deep the water was, as she did sometimes, at Mindon Lake.

Was he trying to catch Mrs. Mint's fish and—hurt them? That would be very cruel. She loved her fish. She even had names for some of them. Mitzi, and Bob, and Water-Baby.

The thought frightened Kit. She made a little protesting move, in her niche among the willows.

Another chuckle, black ripples on the glittering white. The eyes and nose were facing in her direction now.

"Who's that? Who's there?"

His voice, even though it was very low, sounded frightened.

She held her breath. He came out of the pond with a rustling and splashing of water and stood on the grassy bank, listening. To her very great relief, the Mints' cat Margaret jumped up on the bank beside him and meowed in greeting. She heard Laddy let out a long sigh. He reached down and stroked the cat, who withdrew haughtily from his wet hand.

Then he went up the hill to Mrs. Mint's house. It was only by straining her anxious ears that she heard the whisper of a whine as one of the garage doors was opened and then closed.

Pondering on what she had seen, she slipped back onto the terrace, climbed the wall where Lucia had lounged in the morning, seized the drainpipe and pulled herself up.

It was nice, it was very nice, to be back in bed, and to hear Donna's soft companionable breathing, quite near. She was suddenly cold, and pulled up the blue cotton bedspread over the sheet.

If he was standing in the pond to get cool, it was an odd way to go about it. The Mints had a perfectly good shower in their bathroom. Kit admired it, because the tiles were a bright coral, with a little gold flower in the center of each tile, and there was a striped coral-and-gold shower curtain and coral-colored towels; while the Keanes' bathroom was nakedly white.

But people, she had discovered from earliest memory, did do odd things. A lot of the time.

Still pondering, she fell abruptly asleep.

SEVEN

There was a great commotion, which nobody needed, Sunday morning, about Mrs. Mint's plants.

Philip, who had gotten to bed at 5:30, was lying on the living-room sofa with a half-finished cup of coffee, a bottle of aspirin, and the untouched Sunday *Times* within reach. He regarded Sunday as a legal day off unless he was racing against time and under any circumstances, after the night's festivities, would have found his work impossible.

"That's what people don't think about," he said peevishly to Therese. "They come at you and steal your mind blind, they dispose of your next day's work as though it didn't mean a thing. It could cost me a hundred, who knows, a thousand dollars in thinking power. Then they go blithely off to their bank or factory and get their salaries even if they don't lift a finger. It's hard."

He sighed, and thought about a cold lemony whiskey sour.

Therese was not aware of the presence of bankers or factory workers at the Keanes' Saturday night.

"Well, you wouldn't work today, anyway," she said reasonably. "Take your aspirin, Philip. Why didn't you just go to bed and leave them? They never would have noticed. I was asleep by three."

"Therese, do you think you could, mmmm—"

She read his mind with accuracy. "I don't think there are any lemons."

"There's an orange. I'm sure there's one orange."

Mrs. Mint's face appeared in the open top half of the Dutch door.

"Yoohoo," she said without her usual cheeriness. "May I come in?"

Nobody said yes or no and she did come in, followed by Gladys. She cast a quick eager look about the room, as if she expected to see fallen bodies on the rug or behind the chairs. Therese had disposed of the worst of the mess, the glasses and ashtrays and plates of half-eaten food.

"Nice party last night?" She sniffed. "It sounded very merry. All the way over to our house."

"Will you have a cup of coffee?" Therese asked. "I think there's a cup left."

Mrs. Mint examined her: her gray linen dress, sort of the color of her eyes, folded in an ashy cuff against the slender apricot-gold shoulders. Mag Keane, she thought, was a trusting woman to go away and leave her husband alone with her sister. Plain little thing at first, but then you began to notice something . . .

She summoned up the indignation that had brought about her Sunday morning invasion of the house.

"Thanks, but this isn't exactly a social call. Some vandal has been at my garden, tore up some of my finest plants, during the night."

"Well, don't look at *us*, Mrs. Mint," Philip said, and put a hand to his throbbing head.

"I thought it was Laddy, we'd had a bit of a spat," Mrs. Mint went on. "But he swears not. He said he was waked in the night by a noise in the garden and looked out and saw your Mr. Coe ripping away at things. There was a bright moon, he says he was sure it was Mr. Coe."

"I hope and pray he was mistaken," Philip said. At that moment, his eyes, and Therese's, and Gladys's—and finally Mrs. Mint's, as she turned sharply around—happened to focus on a tin pail standing on the hearth. In it were a mass of wilted bright pink phlox, still upright blue lupine, and yellow snapdragon.

"There they are!" Mrs. Mint shrieked. She went over to

the pail. "Ripped up by the roots! That's a cruel thing, that's a nasty thing. My plants. My *plants*."

She snatched a piece of paper lying beside the pail and read in a high outraged voice: "To the widow Vane, all for the love of you."

"Oh, God," Therese said. Philip was speechless.

"Must've made quite a conquest," Mrs. Mint said savagely. "Though, from his handwriting, I'd say he was crocked . . ." She cast an eye at Gladys, and amended this. "Partying it up, he must have been. I'm sure I don't know what to do about the gaping holes in my garden, I'll try to get these back in, look, roots and all . . ."

"I'm sure Johnny didn't know what he was doing," Philip protested feebly. "Thought they were wildflowers . . ."

"I should hope he didn't know what he was doing, healthy growing things, roots and all—"

"If they don't recover," Therese said, feeling a perfectly undeserved guilt, "I'll get some more from a nursery, I promise."

"*My* flowers—all for the love of *you*. I call that nerve."

"What's that noise? That car?" Philip cried.

He got up and looked out one of the back living-room windows, joined by the others.

In the driveway beneath was a Checker cab with New York license plates. As they watched, the cab door opened and Patrick Keane got out and took a number of bills from his wallet.

"Oh no," Philip groaned. "Oh, Christ, what have we done to deserve this? Not even a phone call—oh God, look, he's got *luggage*—"

In unbelieving horror, he saw the driver lift a large leather suitcase from the front seat and, with Patrick Keane, approach the outside back stairway to the kitchen.

Mrs. Mint's rage over her plants was put away for later reference. Her nose quivered and her eyes sparkled. Was there about to be a scene, between the two brothers? Mag Keane had told her that they didn't, occasionally, get on.

Patrick came in through the kitchen and the dining room and just missed stumbling over the step down into the living room.

"That's a murderous step you have there," he said accusingly to Philip. "And for God's sake, have you any idea of the distance you are from New York by cab? It cost me seventy-six dollars on the meter, to say nothing of the tip."

Therese had a falling-away feeling in her stomach; as though it would land on the floor. She sat very still in Philip's wing chair, clasping her hands tightly together.

Patrick gave her his charming wide smile, that lit the bony big face and the brilliant hazel eyes. Yes. They were hazel after all.

"Hello, Therese. Hello, Mrs. Mint, and Gladys, isn't it? I would have called you, Phil, but I had an idea you'd say you were just finishing a book or had a full house or some damned excuse or other, so I just hailed a cab."

"Therese, go make that drink," Philip said desperately.

"How nice," Patrick said, "to have a live-in servant to order about. Where's your uniform, Therese? And your cap?"

"Look here," Philip said, "it's bad enough that you've come at all—I *am* finishing a book and we do have a full house—but if you're going to be contumelious into the bargain—"

Donna and Kit appeared from nowhere. Patrick picked up Kit and kissed her and put a large beautifully formed hand on Donna's head. He took out, as he always did when he visited, silver dollars and gravely presented them to palms politely withheld until the clinking sounded. Seeing Gladys's eyes on him, he gave her a dollar bill for which she thanked him profusely.

"I have strict orders for you kids," he said, "to be observed the entire length of my stay here. If someone named Mrs. Morton calls up and asks for me, I am not here. In fact, if any strange woman asks for me, I'm not here. On the whole, you'd be better off not answering the phone at all."

"Fine," Philip said. "Life at 222 Willen's Road suspended because an uninvited guest arrives. Who the hell is Mrs. Morton?"

"You'll hear more about her. Later."

"That was what I was afraid of. *Therese*—have you no mercy?"

To Mrs. Mint, Patrick Keane sounded fascinatingly like

someone in one of his own plays. Not that she'd seen any of them.

Therese thought that by now her legs ought to be able to support her. She hadn't seen Patrick for at least two years, since the Keanes' Uncle Sergius's funeral in New York, and she was horrified to find the impact his presence had on her.

Had she learned, changed, strengthened so little, acquired so little ownership over herself in the more than six years since she had been told—not by Patrick himself, but by an upset, swearing Mag—that he and Jenny had gotten married, suddenly and secretly, one night the week before?

She had thought the world had come to an end. But, of course, sooner or later you got over these young, awful things. Or did you, in the case of Patrick?

He and Jenny were divorced, by mutual consent, the year she married Jonathan Vane. Patrick was away somewhere at the time of the wedding.

"I'll come and help with whatever you're going to fix to drink," Patrick said. "Or at least advise. How are you, Therese? You've had pneumonia . . .? I didn't find out until later, otherwise I would have come by with grapes."

"I'm fine now," Therese said, squeezing the one orange and paying close attention to her work. "A bit woozy, now and then."

Which would explain, she thought, the faint trembling of her hands.

Using Philip's crock, she measured whiskey, poured in the orange juice, added the remains of a cold bottle of ginger ale for volume, and put in a few drops of Angostura bitters.

"I'll shake it for you." He took the crock and placed a saucer over the top of it and shook it until it foamed.

"Do you still spend a great deal of time in Paris, Patrick?" she asked politely. He kept an apartment in Paris, and Mag said he spent a portion of each year there. A Patrick thing to do.

He was that comparative American rarity, a big tall graceful man of splendid looks and bone and bearing. There was nothing self-conscious or tentative about him; he had a certainty, a balanced ease. His voice was a soft Maryland baritone, deeper and more resonant than Philip's.

"On and off," Patrick said. "The jelly glass for me—no, for Philip. I'll have the mug. The stemmed glass, watch that rim, it's chipped, for you. Mrs. Mint—?"

"She doesn't drink."

His intent gaze made her terribly uncomfortable. What was he looking for? Lines, different contours, the changes life made in a face?

Philip got up from the sofa to get his jelly glass from the old tin beer tray. He saluted Patrick with his drink and said pointedly, "Well, here's to a short stay and a merry one."

"You'll find everything will work out very comfortably," Patrick said in a reassuring way, as if he was the host and not the guest. "I'll take over Mag's studio—"

"Take over is well put."

"—and use your typewriter when you're not using it."

"I use it all morning and I need it all afternoon for notes and corrections. And it's a temperamental machine, I don't want anyone else pounding it to pieces. Hire your own damned typewriter." Then he looked sharply taken aback. "What are we talking about here? Two days, three days? I know you usually have a crowded schedule—"

"Who knows?" Patrick said. "Relax and get your drink down. You look a bit green."

Therese thought that the brothers were fond enough of each other, but that Patrick brought a kind of glisten with him, of money and success, jet planes and international wanderings, that shook Philip in the quiet if insecure way of life he had deliberately chosen and was normally quite happy in. Patrick's presence would make the unpaid bills loom larger, the living-room Oriental even shabbier, the hard work at the typewriter even harder.

Patrick's latest play was to be made into a movie. Philip's pie in the sky, above and beyond the glorious news of a magazine sale (which had only happened once, three books back) was a movie sale.

Mrs. Mint had been hoping to hear about the Mrs. Morton who was to be denied telephone communication with Patrick; but the two men were talking, amiably now, about Mag's travels.

"Well, I must go," she said. "Lunchtime. I suppose you don't mind"—this, archly, with exaggerated politeness, for Patrick's benefit—"if I take my flowers back with me, Therese."

Philip, feeling much revived, gave her a kindly smile.

"Yes, take them, Mrs. Mint. Roots and all."

EIGHT

"How could a person tell if their tea was poisoned?" Kit asked, watching Mrs. Mint, in her kitchen, raising a rose-patterned cup to her lips.

Mrs. Mint started violently and spilled tea into her saucer. Then she took a belated sip and said:

"I call it a shame you're allowed to read those books of your father's and listen to all that hair-raising talk. It's not healthy for a young child. Why should anyone try to poison my tea?"

"I don't know . . ." Kit's eyes assumed a vague look. "But so many things can happen to a person when they're not doing anything bad. Lucia got hit in the head with a stone, last year, on her bicycle . . ."

"Don't go looking for trouble. You made me come all over dizzy for a moment, startling me like that."

"How is your back, where you fell?"

"Sore, inflamed, black and blue, I'll tell you. I had Higgins send that boy up here and I grilled him and he swore and declared he didn't know anything about any butter. Always tell the truth, Kit, it's a wicked world."

Kit drank some of her milk and finished her oatmeal cookie. They were sitting companionably at the kitchen table, which was covered in daisy-printed white oilcloth. The kitchen was dazzlingly clean and smelled of wet dish mop and the wax Mrs. Mint used on her wooden cabinets.

Gladys was upstairs washing her hair. Kit had never seen her sit down to a cup of tea with Mrs. Mint.

"I don't like to hurry you," she said politely, "but we will go see the fish soon?"

"Soon's ever I get this down. Fish, fish, why are you so concerned about my fish all of a sudden?"

Kit's first question, when she arrived early in the afternoon, was, "Are your fish all right, Mrs. Mint?" The way she asked it, and the funny expression on her round milky pink-cheeked face had given Mrs. Mint, she immediately announced, a turn.

Kit had no idea of telling Mrs. Mint that she had seen Laddy in the pond. Mrs. Mint might think he had sneaked out late, to visit Edie Avanti, and stopped for a bathe on the way back. She might fly into a rage. Kit liked her better when she was in a good and confiding temper.

"Now, then, fish it is," Mrs. Mint said, getting the little green box of fish food from one of her cabinets. "Come along."

They knelt side by side on the bank. The flung food freckled the water.

"Come, little fishies," Mrs. Mint sang out. There they were, racing to her.

"How many of them are there? How can you be sure they're all there? Do fish get sick, or can they hurt themselves?"

"Mercy, Kit, nothing but disasters, for you, today. Sometimes one of them sickens and dies, old age. I guess, or bacteria or germs or something. As to how many, close to three dozen, I'd say, give or take a few."

There seemed to be quite a lot of fish, and they were hungrily gobbling, which was reassuring.

"Where's the one with the black marks?" Kit demanded. "Water-Baby. I don't see him."

"Now wait, now wait—there he is," triumphantly. "Honest to God, Kit, you'll have me a nervous wreck. He's one of my pets. He's at least ten years old."

"If someone put poison in the water, how long would the fish take to die?"

"*Kit!*" snapped Mrs. Mint. "That's enough. Run along home. I have things to do."

It was with genuine concern and not in any spirit of interference that she approached Philip later that sunny Sunday afternoon.

He was stretched in a faded striped hammock in the deep shade between a Golden Delicious apple tree and a Baldwin, half-dozing, half-reading the *Times*. The lawn here was close to the Mints' boundary. Mrs. Mint picked her way through wild mustard and wild geranium, mindful of snakes—they might be only garter snakes, but they scared a body with their oozy rustling through the weeds—and stopped a few yards away from Philip.

She cleared her throat. "Philip, none of my business but I thought I'd better speak to you anyway. About Kit."

He sat up abruptly in the hammock and almost fell out. "What about Kit?"

"She's been talking morbid something awful. People's tea being poisoned, and thrown rocks, and something awful happening to my fish, and poison in the pond. It couldn't be good for a seven-year-old child."

"You mean she thinks someone's trying to poison *her*?" Philip frowned.

"No, it's just a blathering, her head's full of death and disaster."

Philip sighed. "It probably doesn't mean a thing. Mag would know what to do, or what not to do . . . very well, Mrs. Mint. I'll have Therese feed her a bland diet of the *Pink, Green,* and *Yellow Fairy Books*—Lang, you know."

Mrs. Mint didn't know. "Books around. Tricky. They will get into them." She herself kept no books around, except an encyclopedia she had bought by installments, and *Reader's Digest* condensed three-in-ones, which she herself didn't read but which looked nice on the shelf in the den, cultural.

And that is just about enough, Philip thought, of Mrs. Mint on child-raising. He lay back and deliberately closed his eyes and said sleepily, "Thanks, Mrs. Mint . . ." and in the act of feigning sleep, soon slept.

Patrick settled himself in Mag's studio. This consisted of unpacking, prowling the house closets for twisted frail wire hangers—he could only find four unused ones—and getting

Lucia to wash a couple of dirty sheets for him. They were drying now over spirea bushes at the back of the house.

He found a couple of cans of cold beer in the refrigerator and appropriated them for what he said was his private house-warming. He gave Lucia his late-lunch order: "Any kind of sandwich, but no cream cheese, no jelly, no peanut butter, and don't cut the crusts off."

Studying his new domain, he wandered about, drinking his beer. Close to the studio, there was a grape arbor, twilit green, with the old well at the end of it. It was still a working well; Philip had wanted to nail the cover down, but you couldn't nail through the soft old wood into the hard stone, and the well was occasionally used when something happened to the water supply at the house, cesspools backing up and other crises, such as the water being briefly cut off because the bill hadn't been paid for months. Philip had to content himself with dire threats to his children about going anywhere near the well.

Patrick lifted the cover and dropped a stone; quite a long time before the hollow sound of the splash. He replaced the cover very carefully.

"You shouldn't go near that well," a voice said, high above his head. He looked up into the apple tree to the right of the grape arbor and saw Donna's dangling bramble-scratched legs and sandaled feet, and the foreshortened thin face above one knee.

He went over and leaned against the trunk.

"What are you doing up there? Besides eating a banana?"

"I like it in trees," Donna said. "But what I'm supposed to be doing is looking for clues. Kit murdered her doll, one of them, this morning, and put clues around about who the real murderer was and I'm supposed to be hunting for them. I thought there might be one up here."

"How did she murder her doll?" Patrick asked, interested.

"Rubbed a peach about its mouth, so it would smell the way a person's breath smells who is killed with cyanide."

"And what kind of clues? Notes?"

"Oh no, real ones. A thread pulled from a torn pocket on a dress of mine, caught on a rosebush near the terrace steps, a smear of Lucia's nail polish where you wouldn't expect to find it—it's a silly kid's game," she added defensively. "But

Kit likes to play it, and she doesn't have anyone young around, so I do.''

"How do you determine who was the murderer when you've found all the clues?"

"See where everybody was at the time of the murder, everybody you've found clues about, and the person who hasn't got an alibi is the one. Of course, we never tell them, if it turns out to be Dad, or Angus or Fay.''

"Don't they wonder why they're being questioned about where they were at the time of the crime?"

"We always put it in a subtle way. They have no idea, really, what we're talking about.''

"Have you found any clues involving your Aunt Therese in this affair?"

"No. Not yet.''

Donna enjoyed talking to Patrick, who was always quite direct with her. She found his presence exhilarating. There was something about him that waked up the sleepy summer, gave it punctuation, and a feeling that things were going to happen, now that he was here.

"Do you like having her to stay?"

"Yes—she's not a bit like Aunt Grace.''

"Oh God, Grace," Patrick said. "Yes. But a good woman, does her duty as she sees it. Tell me, about Therese.''

"Tell you what?"

"What she's like. I haven't seen her for years.''

Donna gazed thoughtfully down at him, charmed with his looks, in a way like her father and in a way so different, and with his white shirt, that was probably linen, and his madras shorts.

("Did you see his legs?" Lucia had asked. "They're fabulous. Like a statue, a Greek statue. And how did they get so brown so early in the summer?"

("Lucia!" Donna was slightly scandalized. "He's our uncle. That's incest.''

("Well," Lucia said airily, "incest must be a thing that happens to people, or there wouldn't be a word for it, would there?'')

She couldn't think of much to tell Patrick, about Therese. "She's nice, and doesn't bother people, and reads a lot. Sometimes she sings to herself while she's cleaning, or making her bed—oh, and Johnny Coe likes her. He tore Mrs. Mint's garden to pieces last night, for her.'' Donna giggled.

"Is she—does she have a man, calling her up, coming around?''

"A man called her yesterday, from her magazine in New York, someone named Bowers, I suppose it was about work but she was laughing . . . or, a boy friend, do you mean? No, I don't think so. She's a *widow,*'' Donna explained, innocently pronouncing sentence.

"Don't tell her I was asking about her, there's a good girl. She would think it wasn't polite. And,'' he added firmly, "it isn't.''

"There's a lot of murdering and poisoning going on around here,'' Patrick said to Philip.

They were having a pre-drinks drink while they waited for Therese, who was taking a bath.

Philip looked worried again. "Has Kit been at you? About the poisoned fish, and the stones, and the tea?''

"No, Donna—but it was Kit, she said, who murdered her doll. With a peach.''

"I don't suppose it amounts to anything. Think of the things we were up to. My God, sometimes I wonder how we ever grew up alive. You, stealing Aunt Bea's car when you were seven and driving off down the hill—''

"—and you, practicing shooting, when I was up in the pine tree hiding because of some frightful thing I did, I can't remember what, bullets whistling past my head—''

"In any case, I got a lecture from Mrs. Mint, about Kit. It's a phase, as they say. Maybe I'll start another phase going. Get them to sweat out their fantasies with some honest labor. Suppose you give a prize to whoever has the best garden in one week's time.''

"All right,'' Patrick said. "Five dollars for the best garden. Let's only hope they don't resemble well-cared-for cemetery plots.''

NINE

It was after one o'clock in the morning, and Patrick lay peacefully asleep in Mag's studio.

The sudden flinging open of the unlocked screen door waked him. He shot upright and pulled the cord over the bed that switched on the naked light bulb.

"What the hell—"

"Who are you?" the woman asked, panting. They gazed at each other, Patrick yawning, the woman continuing to pant.

"Fay," he said. "Fay MacPherson."

"Philip's brother Peter."

"Patrick."

They had met once at a party, years ago.

"Is there anything I can do for you?" Patrick asked. "I'm rather busy sleeping."

She looked with interest at his broad bare shoulders under the sheet and his roughened hair.

"I don't suppose you have a drink out here? But first things first. I left Angus tearing the house apart looking for my manuscript. I'm writing a book about him and it makes him self-conscious and I'm terriby afraid he'll destroy it. It's an irreplaceable documentary account of his life and ways and his very *being*. I've hidden it here and I just wanted to be sure it was safe, not getting moldy or with ants at it or something."

"There's no chance he'll come after you, is there?" Patrick asked in alarm. He had heard about Angus's temper.

"I don't think so, he'll be searching for hours, it's a big house—ah. Safe and dry." She waved the folder at him and replaced it, under the bust of Kit, carefully draping the green cloth.

"Can't you hide it somewhere else?"

"You wouldn't want him rampaging through your brother's house, would you, terrifying everybody? And now, if you do have a drink, I'm rather in need of it, my heart's pounding, feel my pulse and you'll see—" She held out a strong plump arm to Patrick. Her fingers curved against his cheek.

"I'd forgotten," she said, "what a really very beautiful man you are."

Patrick forbore feeling her pulse. He supposed he might as well humor her; her animal vitality crackled around the room and now he was thoroughly awake. He got up, knotting his sheet at his waist, and took his emergency bottle of scotch out of the leather suitcase. Fay sat down on the bed and watched him with open pleasure and appreciation.

She was wearing a sweater and a flowered cotton skirt which she managed to make look like anything but casual country clothing. He noticed the scratches on her long richly curved legs.

Mag kept a little eating and drinking equipment on one of the windowsills, a few glasses and spoons and plates and a battered aluminum pot to boil coffee water in. He poured her a drink, added water at her request, at the sink in the corner of the room, and gave it to her.

"Aren't you going to join me? Please do. It's rather a wonderful feeling, alone and awake in the country night when the house over there is asleep. I believe people should break patterns more than they do, collect new feelings, cherish them—"

She patted the bed beside her. Patrick made a drink for himself and sat down on the straight chair.

"Here's to your work in progress," he said.

There was a sudden thrashing and swearing as someone charged into the head-high blackberry bushes near the studio door. Then the door itself was thrown open.

They're a great couple for panting, Patrick thought.

Angus MacPherson, his chest heaving, stood for a few seconds in the doorway, mute and staring. He was a short powerful man, ruddy-colored, with red-fair hair over a high knobby forehead and brilliant blue eyes burning now with astonished rage. The eyes went from Partick in his sheet to Fay, transfixed, sitting on the bed.

Before Patrick knew what was coming, he was struck a tremendous blow on the edge of his jaw and his chair and he with it crashed over sideways. Angus seized Fay by her hair and pulled her upright.

"You're hurting me," she screamed.

"Wench," Angus panted. "Whore."

"I only stopped by for a friendly drink," Fay cried. "You've probably broken Philip's brother's jaw. I hardly know the man. How did you know I was here?"

Patrick had picked himself up. With one hand, he felt his jaw to see if it was intact; with the other, he selected a large chunk of marble with a sharp jagged edge.

Angus had been an engineer on a Scottish merchant ship; now, in his early fifties, he was still tough as iron. And Patrick didn't care to use his fists—he might need his hands for typing, if his mission here extended any length of time.

"If you are planning to do away with your wife," he said to Angus, "I'd appreciate it if you'd go somewhere else to get on with it."

"Don't leave me alone with him," Fay shrieked. "Tell him we've done nothing, nothing, but share a drink in the night—"

"All right. We've done nothing, nothing," Patrick said. "And now for Chirst's sake get out of here, MacPherson, and let me get back to sleep. If I can, that is—my jaw is killing me."

Philip appeared at the door.

"What's going on here? Angus woke me up trying to pound the front door down, looking for you, Fay, I said you weren't here, I didn't know you were visiting Patrick—"

"She wasn't visiting me," Patrick said indignantly. "She'd forgotten a—sweater she'd left here the last time she came to see Mag"—Fay threw him a grateful glance—"and I felt like a drink and gave her one."

"The wench fled," Angus growled between his teeth. "Fled while I was searching the house for something she'd hidden.

Took her car. I looked for her in the bar at the corner but it was closed. I figured this would be the next port of call, and drove over. I saw a light in the studio after I left your house and found them drinking and carrying on and this fellow in his sheet—''

He made a belligerent move toward Patrick, who raised his chunk of marble threateningly. Philip seized Angus's arm.

"Bed, everybody,'' he said. "No harm done, except my sleep destroyed and probably my workday ruined tomorrow, not that anybody cares. I'll just have a short drink, Patrick, and then we'll all clear out. Angus, this is my brother. Have you met? I don't remember. My younger brother.''

"Aye,'' Angus said. "The drawing room—and bedroom—playwright.'' He spat the scornful words.

"Yes, we've met,'' Patrick said. "You're the man who throws things at his wives. Oh, and I believe you write. Novels. Sea yarns.''

As Angus MacPherson was a writer of international reputation and acclaim, this was severe.

The word "yarns'' threatened to rearouse his ebbing rage. Philip finished his drink in one gulp and led him away, and saw the two safely into their cars. Fay's was parked in the driveway where it curved around a great clump of lilacs, concealing it from the casual, or Angus', view.

As they accelerated, backed and filled and shouted at each other out of their car windows, Fay could be heard saying,

"You first! You're not going to ram *me* from behind like a bloody oil tanker after a yacht.''

Therese was waiting at the top of the stairs, bundled into a white robe.

"What was all that shouting and commotion? Is Patrick all right?''

Philip, halfway up the stairs, rubbed his eyes and paused to consider.

"Now that you ask me, I don't exactly know what it was all about. Patrick seems okay, I doubt if his jaw is broken. He and Fay were drinking out there and Angus stumbled on them. God, another day shot to hell. Excuse me, Therese, I must get to sleep before I really wake up.''

Therese was left to herself to try to sort out Patrick's inexplicably unbroken jaw, Fay, the drinks in the studio, and the invectives echoing across the soft summer night.

Well, people don't change, she thought, darkly and sadly, Patrick doesn't. And neither do I.

TEN

Therese had firmly announced that she would take her week in the kitchen, turn and turn about. Today was her first day on duty.

This, she thought indignantly in midafternoon, isn't a task, it's a career.

People drifted in and out and made themselves things to eat and drink at any hour. There was no formal lunch, but sandwiches and various snacks had been prepared and eaten and cleaned up after, by her. Now, there were the remains of someone's egg salad—the mayonnaise jar was empty, she must remember to put it on the shopping list—and a trail of spilled coffee across the gray linoleum, probably from Philip's mug, and half a bread-and-jam sandwich sitting on a windowsill with flies buzzing about it. More dishes in the sink, and a milk glass. And what kind soul had thoughtfully collected every overflowing ashtray in the house and deposited them all on the round oak kitchen table?

In the course of tidying up, she heard the voices under the window facing her as she stood at the sink.

Donna and Kit, reading their stories to each other.

When the mood struck them, they worked at the dining-room table, silently scribbling in pencil on yellow paper taken from Philip's supplies. Therese didn't like to pry and hadn't discovered whether they worked at novels, or short stories, or their informal diaries, or what.

Donna's literary undertaking seemed to be about a cat named Harriet, who lived in a house that sounded remarkably like the Keanes'. The cat got lost and wandered up a great long driveway past a gatehouse. There was a good deal about butlers, and swimming pools, and maids, and money, and a girl of eleven who had a closet jammed with new dresses. Harriet was adopted by the rich family as their house cat, but she had no duties as there were no mice or rats. Apparently she was to start on a life of luxury.

". . . and that's all I have now," Donna said. "Your turn, Kit. Don't cheat and make things up while you're reading."

Kit's story was about a woman named Mrs. Mountain. Therese, running water into the sink, missed some of it.

". . . and he gave her a push. And she fell into the water, and couldn't swim. And she drowned. The fish swam through her hair and tried to wake her up and gave her little kisses on her cheeks but she didn't wake up—you know how they make little sucking kissing shapes with their mouths, Donna, when their fish food is thrown out—"

In the sunny kitchen, a coldness brushed Therese.

Donna said, "I think that's a perfectly horrible story. It's one thing to murder your doll, she isn't real and she can't feel and in her own way she's still alive, and always will be, but Mrs. Mint—"

"Not Mrs. Mint. Mrs. Mountain. She's *made up,*" Kit said. "Your Harriet is made up. There isn't any cat named Harriet here."

"You're still going on and on about Laddy. I thought that was just a silly idea you had. I thought you'd forgotten all about it."

"There isn't any Laddy in the story. His name is Percy."

"Percy, Percy, Mountain, Mountain, it's Laddy and Mrs. Mint."

"And so there, you're Harriet. And you don't like it here and you'd like to live somewhere else, and leave Dad and Dementia and Aunt Therese and me. And Lucia."

"Good afternoon." Patrick's voice under the window, amiable. "Am I too late to hear the readings?"

Donna's embarrassed mumble, "It's just our stories, we only read them to each other. Does your jaw still hurt?"

"Frightfully. Angus is lucky he wasn't heaved down the well—" Therese could hear the hanging pause, and sense his wish that he hadn't said that, to the Keane children.

"—or," he amended, "had his shandygaff cut off for at least six months."

"Did he knock any of your teeth out?" Kit asked with vivid interest.

"No. And that's enough of that. Time to get cracking. I am authorized by your father to pay—out of my own pocket, naturally—five dollars to whoever has the best floral display in her garden in one week's time. That would be, let's see, by exactly two forty-five next Monday afternoon. Exhibits will be judged on neatness, profusion of bloom, well-watered soil and other things I haven't thought up yet. And no stealing stuff out of Lucia's garden, even though she doesn't give it much of her attention any more."

His proposal was greeted with enthusiasm. In a wrangle about who was to have the first use of the hoe, the voices faded.

There was only the oriole singing, in the *Grimes Golden* apple tree where the swing hung motionless on its ropes.

"And she fell into the water, and couldn't swim. And she drowned . . ."

What would Mag do? Should she say anything to Philip about it? Tattletale Aunt Therese, chilled by fantasies on a summer afternoon. She could hear the whispers. Don't ever say anything in front of her, or that she can overhear, ever.

No. The cold little moment had gone. The kitchen, at least for an hour or so, was neat again. Time to drift along with doctor's orders, and have a lazy, floaty nap . . .

Nevertheless, she was glad to see, late in the day, Kit sitting on the bottom terrace step. Playing, with great concentration, jacks.

She sat on the top step and Patrick was beside her, his head propped on one elbow, the length of his body lazily extended to allow one bare foot to rest on the grass.

The stones of the step were uneven and Kit had provided herself with the rusted old beer tray as a playing field. She looked entirely absorbed and happy as she bounced her little red ball and seized her jacks.

There was a great mottled blue and purple bruise on the right side of Patrick's jaw. She looked at it with concern.

"It was not a bacchanalian orgy, out there in the studio last night, there were no fun and games or adulterous acts performed," he said, "—since you're too polite to ask. Fay was checking on her manuscript and Angus thought what you are probably thinking, and dive-bombed me."

She felt him uncomfortably close. She moved away a little as though she was just shifting to a more relaxed position and took a cold sip of her gin and tonic.

Inside the house, the telephone rang.

"I'm not here and I'm not expected," Patrick called.

She wasn't sure she thoroughly believed in Mrs. Morton, but it was something to talk about. She still wasn't at all at home with him but she might as well sound as if she was.

"Tell me about your Mrs. Morton."

"She's a redhead," Patrick answered instantly. "She rents the place in Paris the eight months or so I'm not renting it. She seems to feel this constitutes some sort of emotional contract between us. She's a determined kind of woman. She's gone through two husbands. Now she wants to rent my apartment in New York the four months *I'm* away, and to marry me, I suppose, along with the joint signing of the lease."

"And you don't want to marry her?"

"No." He reached over and took her hand. "Why are we talking like two strangers at a cocktail party? I want to know all about you, Therese, it's been a long time."

She thought he had no right to her hand—the enfolding so warm and casual, so electric. When she was twenty-three, she had an idea he was going to marry her. He hadn't.

She felt her hand begin to tremble, inside his. She took it away.

"*Terrezz,*" he teased her, just as he had used to, long ago. "Your mother must have been reading too many French novels."

And, just as she had used to, she said, "Well, it's better than being named after a parade."

And thought, as she had before, that that was one of the troubling things about him: he was, in his way, a one-man parade.

The telephone rang again. Donna came out on the terrace.

"It's for you, Aunt Therese. From Dublin. From *Ireland*." She sounded impressed.

It was Beau Bowers, the art director on *You* whom she had been seeing a good deal of in the spring and whom she thought that sometime—and perhaps—she might marry. She found him amusing, and endearing. On the phone, he told her how much he missed her, described his day shooting a fashion feature, Green Grows Your Wardrobe, in Phoenix Park, which made her laugh a lot. He said he'd bought her some tweed, very thin and fine, that matched her eyes. And he sent her kisses and all his love.

Patrick hadn't moved. "Dublin?" Polite curiosity.

"An art director on the magazine. Beau Bowers." She smiled reminiscently at the Phoenix Park tales.

"Those people shouldn't call you on business," he said severely. "You're an invalid. Although I must say you sounded amused."

"It wasn't a business call."

Patrick held up his gin and tonic to the light. It blazed silver, tiny beads of bubbles winking on the lime quarter at the bottom.

"Naturally," he said. "Naturally, there would be a man."

His voice sounded far away, abstracted. As though, she thought, he was thinking something out, working on the plot of one of his plays.

ELEVEN

Gladys Mint knelt on her bed and looked out the window at the light rain.

She was at loose ends. She had, unasked, cleaned the coral and gold bathroom in a warm glow of virtue, and now would have liked to play pinochle with Donna and Kit. But they had gone off somewhere with their aunt, in the car. She thought it was mean of them not to have asked her along. Kit was a tag-along kid to be put up with, but Donna was her only real companion, in summer.

Mrs. Mint had grumblingly driven over to see to her sister-in-law Rosemary, who was in bed with a bad cold and needed errands done and food fixed for her.

Laddy was at work. The house was very still. There would be no one to see her if . . .

She told herself that it would be a kind and thoughtful act. Whatever Kit had hidden under the stone at the edge of her garden might get wet, soaked, in the rain, probably disintegrate. It might be dollar bills, which could conceivably rot. Besides, she was burning with a special curiosity. Kit had kept turning her head to peer at the Mints' house while she was hiding whatever it was.

Gladys went down the back stairway from the kitchen and through the open garage doors into the warm thin rain. She forded the wild geraniums and mustard that led to the Keanes' lawn, gave the hammock an absent-minded push, and sauntered idly—just in case someone in the Keane house was looking out of a window, Mr. Keane or his brother who was visiting, and whom she found formidable, although she didn't know the word—toward Kit's garden.

A great many weeds had been tugged up and the garden looked somewhat naked. Her back to the house, she bent, unerringly lifted the right stone, found the folded paper and slipped it into her pocket. She rose casually, pulled up an overlooked ragweed and threw it over the stone wall into the road.

Still on stage for any unseen viewer, and acting the part of innocence, she put her nose to a lavender cosmos. No scent. She went out through the gate opening in the wall, and walked the short distance down the steeply slanting road and into the Mints' driveway.

In her room, with the door closed, she read Kit's notes. Funny way of writing; but with a little effort Gladys could make it out.

Her eyes widened as she read. She was delightfully horrified. How could anyone think her mother would say things like that? Use words like that? Have, even, thoughts like that?

Or maybe it was from one of Kit's stories. But her mother did hate Edie so . . .

". . . trash trash, no better than a hoar as may be you have found out. Mrs. M. . ."

". . . Green love sick kid running after a wop after all the rest have done with her. Mrs. M. . ."

". . . I'll kill you if you don't leave off Edie. L.M. . ."

Her mother, her own mother—well, stepmother—who talked darkly about probable loose goings-on at the Keane house, and among the guests who flocked there.

And, "Now there's that Patrick, probably no better than he should be, divorced, I hear, and a young woman alone in the house, and Philip Keane is not *my* idea of a chaperone—"

Her mother, who said, "Inside our walls, thank God, we're all clean good God-fearing people . . ."

It was all made up, what Kit had written. It was wicked.

It seemed hours before her mother's car turned in at the driveway and disappeared into the garage.

"Yoohoo," Mrs. Mint called, coming up the steps to the kitchen. "Anybody home? Gladys?"

"I'm here, Mother."

"I'm going to have myself a good hot cup of tea. Your Aunt Rosemary makes out to be helpless and she's hardly got a fever at all, 101 at the most, pretends she can't keep anything in her stomach, wanted milk toast and they were out of bread and I had to drive to Mint's to get a loaf, and of course she had no loose cash in the house, she's so afraid of burglars, so whose pocket did the bread come out of?"

"Mother," Gladys said, "I went out for a bit, but Donna and Kit were away with their aunt—"

"Why didn't they take you along? I call that unkind."

"—anyway, I found this piece of paper, lying in the driveway. I thought you'd dropped your grocery list. It's something Kit wrote and it's supposed to be about you and Laddy and it's crazy—"

"Give it here," Mrs. Mint said.

Kit thought it was time for her regular daily check on Mrs. Mint.

They had had a nice morning. As the larder, Aunt Therese said, was somewhat bare, they went to Mint's store and bought all kinds of things they usually didn't have around, four kinds of cheese, Delmonico steaks and Canadian bacon, English water crackers, almond-stuffed olives, apricot and peach preserves, and a great deal of fresh fruit. The two girls were allowed to pick out any delicacies they fancied.

"Be careful, don't spend too much," Donna whispered to Kit. "It's her money, I think. Dad would never have twenties and twenties to give her . . ."

Kit settled for a box of chocolate cookies and a small bag of potato chips. She comfortably munched the chips as she wandered down the slope, passed the willows, and looked to see if Mrs. Mint was feeding her fish. She must be in the house, her car was in the garage. The rain had stopped but the air was still damp and watery-feeling.

She knocked politely at the door at the top of the kitchen stairs. No one answered. As she had every reason to be perfectly confident of the freedom of Mrs. Mint's house, she opened the door and went into the kitchen. A tap dripped. A washed teacup and saucer sat on the drainboard.

There was a sound, a sort of gasp, from the open door of the den, across the little hall beyond the kitchen. Mrs. Mint stood there, her face working, and from nowhere a stab of first terror pierced Kit.

"I came to see how you are today, Mrs. Mint."

"Liar!" screamed Mrs. Mint. "Dirty little foul-mouthed lying wretch!"

She took a few steps forward. For a moment, Kit couldn't move.

"Nasty rotten traitor of a kid! Sucking up to me, eating my cookies and drinking my milk, and all the time spying, writing things down, no doubt for your father and all those people to laugh at and maybe put into one of his books!"

Kit started to back up. Her foot caught the leg of a kitchen chair and she almost fell.

"Get out of here!" Mrs. Mint screamed. "Get out of here and never come back!" She took another threatening step forward. Kit's mind was quite numb. This couldn't be Mrs. Mint. She had heard about the tantrums, and the temper, and the screaming, but they had never before been turned on her, and she hadn't quite believed any of it. Mrs. Mint was her friend and confidante as well as, at the moment, her responsibility.

"Well, *get*, you dirty little beast, or I'll beat the tar out of you, I swear to God I will—"

Now she came forward in a rush, her arms swinging dangerously. Kit turned and tore the door open. She ran down the stairs. Rags and tatters of hysterical rage poured down the stairs after her.

". . . never again, do you hear? Never this house, never set a foot on this property, sneaking dirty brat—"

She fell headlong down the last three steps, picked herself up without noticing or feeling the skinned knees, and ran down the driveway and into the road, where a car accelerating up the hill just barely missed her and she was, unhearing, sworn at.

Gasping, and crying wildly, she ran, and ran, and ran.

Gladys Mint, who had been hiding, listening, around a bend in the stairs leading up from the hall, hugged herself in terror and a lovely sense of power. That would teach Kit Keane to put all those bad words in her mother's mouth and all those bad thoughts in her head.

She decided that it would be a good thing if she slipped upstairs and stayed in her bedroom for a while until things cooled off.

"Gladys?" A croaking voice, from the kitchen. "I've come all over dizzy. Are you still there?"

Gladys instinctively knew that it wouldn't do, to have her mother know she'd heard her, screaming at Kit. Kit was only, after all, seven years old.

She tiptoed to her bedroom and lay down on her bed and pretended to be neatly and peacefully asleep.

When Laddy Mint got home from Elder's Garage, about six, he found Gladys playing patience on the kitchen table. There was no sign of a dinner in preparation. The Mints usually had dinner as soon as his workday was over.

He saw the closed door into the den. When Mrs. Mint had one of her dizzy spells, or one of her tempers, or in general didn't feel well, she would always lie down on the old couch in the den as she didn't want to crush the cushions in her living room.

"What's wrong with her?" he asked, with a jerk of his head at the den door.

"I guess she doesn't feel well."

"What am I supposed to do—starve?"

"There's some cans of soup in the cupboard." Gladys, unlike the Keanes, had not been encouraged to learn how to fend for herself in the kitchen. Mrs. Mint thought it wasn't ladylike.

Laddy got out a can of tomato soup and opened it. He banged about searching for the right size pot like an angry cook.

"Nothing set her off?"

"Oh, yes—she found a note someone had written, Kit I think, telling about a crazy fight between her and you, putting in all the words."

Laddy's back was to her. He stopped stirring the can of water into the soup.

"What was the fight supposed to be about?"

"Edie. Of course, she must have made it up, all those bad words." Gladys kept her face very solemn.

"Where's the note?"

"She burned it in the sink and washed it all down the drain."

"You read it too?" His back was still turned to her. He had resumed stirring his soup, slowly.

"Not to say read it. I saw a word or two. She snatched it away from me. I guess she took it seriously, you should have heard what she yelled at Kit." She told him. "But anyway, it's all made up, how would Kit know what you and she said to each other, in private like?"

"That's true," Laddy said. "They're always writing those stories of theirs. I heard them once, reading them to each other. I can't eat this whole can of soup, there's a cup for you, Glad, if you want it."

The den door opened and Mrs. Mint emerged. Her eyes and her nose were red, the way she always looked when she had been crying.

She greeted them with mutters and was making a cup of tea when the telephone rang.

"I'll get it," Laddy said.

Mrs. Mint roused herself sufficiently to snap, "Think it's your Edie, maybe. *I'll* get it."

It was Rosemary again. She was sure her temperature had gone up. She had expected her brother, John Mint, home from Bridgeport but he had called to say he was going to stay over and go fishing with the friend he was visiting, early next morning. She, Rosemary, would be all alone. Could Mrs. Mint come over for a while and see if the doctor should be called? And if he was called, fix the bed so it looked decent, it was all damp and rumpled . . .

Mrs. Mint and Rosemary had a hearty dislike for each other, but in the country fashion briefly laid this aside in case of emergency.

"Oh, all right, s'pose there's no way out of it," Mrs. Mint said grimly. "I'm not well myself but we can't both turn ourselves into invalids, can we?"

To the air around her, as she drank her tea, she said, "Trouble, trouble, nothing but trouble today."

TWELVE

Kit wasn't missed until close to dinnertime.

Philip sat at the kitchen table with his martini and watched hungrily as Therese, with an occasional absentminded sip at her drink, trimmed the Delmonico steaks and made salad and beat up a batch of Cheddar cheese biscuits.

He said suddenly, "It all looks very good, Therese, but I owe Mints a hell of a lot, should we really be eating so lavishly?"

"My treat tonight. It's my birthday."

"Oh, God, I forgot." He went over and kissed her. "Happy birthday. I expect a check some time this week, from the paperback people, in fact I should have had it already. Then we'll see."

"Do we expect Patrick to dinner?"

"I fear so," Philip said austerely. "He's gone off to Elder's about hiring a car. Now that does sound bad to me. Who would need a car for a few days' visit? He can always use mine when you and I aren't using it."

"I'm afraid I told him about Elder's. Laddy Mint was trying to get me to hire a car from them . . ." She put her head a little on one side. "Kit won't eat a whole steak, Donna either. I'll split one between them. Oh—Donna. Set the table for me, will you? And, no, I don't think that pear—you'll spoil your dinner."

"I thought Kit would be out here, with you," Donna said.

69

"She must still be over at Mrs. Mint's."

"Call her up or go get her," Philip ordered. "Once these steaks go in, we will brook no interruptions or delays. Hold up on them, Therese, until the lost sheep turns up, or lamb."

At first, no one was alarmed. People came and went, in the house; the dinner hour was flexible, particularly during the long bright June evenings, when sometimes they ate as late as 8:00 or 8:30.

Donna telephoned the Mints and was told by Gladys that Mrs. Mint wasn't there, but over taking care of Rosemary. No, Kit had not gone over there with her. She had come to see Mrs. Mint in the afternoon, and left almost immediately. No, she didn't say where she was going.

Therese, who had been favored recently with Philip's lecture about the fearful dangers of life in the so-called peace and quiet of the country, mentally ran through the list of awful hazards he had named.

Patrick returned, driving the blue Buick convertible.

They scattered to search the grounds for Kit. Philip, pale, went first to the well to see if the cover was on and then looked in the studio, even under the bed. Patrick shouted, "Kit, Kit!" at the top of his lungs, standing on the terrace steps; he could certainly be heard as far away as the other side of Mint's Hill.

Therese smelled her biscuits and went and got them out and said helplessly to Philip, who came running up the outside back stairway, "What now? Does she often do this, just disappear?"

"No—I told you they came around like dogs, at dinnertime— I'll get the car and run up and down the roads around here. She could be picking flowers for Mrs. Mint or talking to the people who live down by the cemetery, they've taken a fancy to her."

She wasn't anywhere, up and down the road.

"She couldn't be hiding?" Patrick asked Donna. "Some kind of new game?"

"Maybe," Donna said, "but I don't think so. I don't think she would."

By concentrating on where she herself would go if for some reason she didn't want anyone to find her, it was Donna who finally found Kit.

She was under the bridge near the waterfall. She lay on her

back in the long soft grass, eyes closed—all sprawled out like her murdered doll, Donna thought in a frightful flash. And for a moment she did think Kit was dead. There was vomit in the grass near her head. Her dress was soiled and torn and her knees bloody, her face dirty and stained with tears and terribly pale.

Donna fell on her knees to the grass and took the limp arm. "Kit—wake up—"

The round blue-gray eyes opened wide. Kit yawned, stared, and then remembered. Her face crumpled into distress but no tears came. Donna tried to lift her but she was too heavy for her to carry.

"Can you walk?—Here, take my hand—What did you do, fall down and hurt yourself and burst out crying and then go to *sleep*. Hurry, Kit—they're all half crazy worrying about you, poor Dad even thought you were down the well—"

Holding Kit tightly by the hand, she dragged her, exhorting speed, over the buttercup meadow, past Mrs. Mint's fishpond, and the willows. She had begun calling, as loud as she could, from a distance and Philip came running at the sound of her voice and snatched Kit up in his arms a little past the stand of willows.

"It's all right, she looks awful, but I think she just hurt herself somehow and cried and fell asleep," Donna said hastily, worried by the pallor of her father's face.

"I think she'd be best off in bed. Would you like to go to bed, Kit?"

"Yes . . . ." She pressed her face deep into his shoulder and shuddered.

"No talking now. Explanations later."

He carried her into the house and up to her room. With Therese's help, she was gently sponged clean; Philip produced antiseptics and bandaging, and waited wincingly for the shriek when the antiseptic touched the raw spots on her knees. No sound came. Kit seemed to be somewhere far away. They covered her with her sheet and two blankets, which stopped the shivering.

"Shock, I think," Philip muttered to Therese. "Will you call Munson? I'll stay here with her."

Dr. Munson, a little later, said, "Nothing to worry about.

Apparently she had a run-in with that Mint woman.'' He was pleased, he said, to see that she no longer looked or sounded remote but was fairly spitting with indignation and righteous rage, said all she was trying to do was help Mrs. Mint. ''She'll sleep it off.''

''That bitch,'' Philip said, and made a move toward the telephone. ''I'll have a word with her—''

Donna reminded him that Mrs. Mint was taking care of her sister-in-law.

''In the morning, then,'' Philip said blackly.

With lost appetites, they sat down to Therese's birthday dinner.

''Now that everybody is tucked in,'' Patrick said, ''we will celebrate the day.''

He had driven into Bedford and come back with four bottles of champagne, and a large tin of Beluga caviar.

''Of course you're not hungry yet but you will be at midnight. For a change of scene, let's go out to my studio.''

''*Your* studio!'' Philip said.

''And for you, Therese—'' Patrick handed her a little square box and bent and kissed her on the top of her head.

A slender, elegant bamboo-patterned gold bracelet lay glistening on its cotton wool.

''How did you know?'' Therese asked, alight with surprise and pleasure. ''How did you remember?''

''I just did,'' Patrick said. ''And the liquor store happened to have champagne glasses, if someone will be kind enough to rinse them out.''

Donna, lying in bed, heard the rustling of a sheet.

''Kit—are you awake?''

''Yes . . .''

''Do you hurt?''

''Not much.''

''What was the fight about, with Mrs. Mint?''

Kit told her.

''All that about foul-mouthed, and lying, and spying, and writing things down—could she have seen your story? Where she drowned and the fish were swimming through her hair?''

"No. It's under my pillow."

"Is there anything else you've written down?"

"Yes, a quarrel, with Laddy, when he said he'd kill her."

"Why did you write it down?"

"As evidence," Kit said from the darkness, "in case he did."

"And where is it?"

"In my garden. Under a stone."

"I'll look in the morning and see if it's still there," Donna said, and fell asleep.

Some time later, she was startled awake. Her heart was pounding. Had it been a dream? Or had it really happened?

That high sudden cry, *"Lad-dee!"*

The bedroom still seemed to echo with it.

Or, maybe she had dreamed it. It wasn't repeated. A bullfrog was croaking somewhere, a gulping ugly noise, but peaceful, normal. A light breeze stirred the leaves of the hickory branches.

Listening tensely, she heard something odd about the silence: no sound of breathing from the other bed. She switched on the lamp on the table beside her bed. Kit's bed was empty. Bathroom, probably. She switched it off and waited.

If it had been a dream, it couldn't have been a nice one. Not, ending as it did, in that somehow awful cry.

Kit didn't come back to bed.

Oh, no, not again, Donna thought wearily. She looked out of the casement window. The living-room lights were on, so the grownups couldn't be in bed; but there was no sound of voices, laughter. The light went considerably beyond the terrace steps before it was lost in the night. She could see no sign of Kit. But, having been so badly frightened today—yesterday?—would she go out alone in the dark?

Maybe to see if her piece of paper, about the quarrel, was still there.

Or maybe she was sleepwalking again.

She was just trying to summon up the courage to go out and look for Kit when she saw the small nightgowned figure drift out of the darkness and move quietly, composedly, up the terrace steps.

She held her breath. Her mother always said, "Don't startle her awake."

Footsteps in the hall, now, outside the open bedroom door.

In the faint reflected light from below, she saw Kit come silently in, get into bed, pull up her sheet and blankets. Donna found something shivery about it all.

She wished she could hear the voices, downstairs.

She went suddenly and deeply back to sleep.

Watching and waiting in his bedroom, with the light out, Laddy Mint, too, saw the small white ghost.

THIRTEEN

Philip, at his typewriter, gratefully drank his first mug of strong black coffee, lit a cigarette, and retyped the last page he had finished, to get his mind working.

Then he remembered he was supposed to be raising hell with Mrs. Mint. He had looked in on Kit when he got up, at seven. She woke when he bent over her. She was milky and rosy and looked perfectly well, warm with sleep and safety. The alarm and recollection dawned in the large beautiful eyes.

"It's a nice day," Philip murmured. "After your breakfast, you might get in some work on your garden. Mind your knees."

His voice woke Donna. She sat up suddenly in her bed and he in turn was alarmed at the expression on her face.

"Is everything all right?" Donna asked. "Is everybody all right?"

"Everything's fine," Philip said. "See that Kit eats a decent breakfast, since she skipped her dinner."

He typed a new paragraph, got up to stalk his workroom for a bit, stroked Peg's head and filled her dish with sunflower seeds, and decided not to ruin the morning's work; he would put off raising hell with Mrs. Mint until early afternoon.

From the studio, he heard a faint, uneven clacking. Patrick, at a typewriter. He must have rented one when he hired the blue Buick. The noise jarred and inhibited Philip in his own effort to think himself through the next two or three pages to

Chapter 12. He went and slammed down the window looking toward the studio. Peg commented, softly for her, *"Por Dios."*

Kit, after breakfast, went immediately to her garden and found that her evidence was indeed missing. This made her feel much better about yesterday, which already had wrapped itself in the aura of an unreal, bad dream.

Naturally Mrs. Mint would be mad at her, if she had read it. She would have no way of knowing that she, Kit, had written it all down for Mrs. Mint's protection. Well, not protection, really, but in case something happened to Mrs. Mint, the police would have something to go on.

The stolen or lost paper suggested a possibility, some time in the future, of Mrs. Mint's being friends with her again.

Gladys Mint was having what her mother called a good lie in bed. She waked first a little after dawn, and took the wax stopples out of her ears. The noise of the bullfrogs, at night, maddened her, but in summer she liked to hear the morning noises, people getting up and moving around, with duties to attend to, while she could turn over luxuriously and go back to sleep.

A clatter from the kitchen window, below hers. Laddy, getting his breakfast. She could hear him whistling to himself. Her mother must be sleeping late, too. Normally, she would fry Laddy's egg and fix his toast and pour him a glass of milk. "Coffee's bad for the nerves. Though I s'pose once you get to that garage of yours you swill it down by the bucket, behind my back. Well, in this house you'll eat right and live right."

She must have gotten home from Rosemary's late; she hadn't arrived back when Gladys went obediently to bed at ten, even though there was nobody to command her to do it.

Hunger finally levered Gladys from her bed. She washed and dressed and went down to the kitchen. Listening sharply for any sounds from above, she indulged in her one disobedience: she gulped the rest of last night's tunafish salad, accompanied by a large glass of grape soda. She hurried to wash out her dish and glass; her mother wouldn't approve.

"Do you want to ruin your lovely skin, Gladys? People are what they eat, I always say. Eat healthy and you'll look healthy and be healthy. It's as simple as that.''

She looked out the kitchen window to see if there were any Keanes on view. Kit, standing beside her garden, holding an old tin watering can high. No sign of Donna.

Ten minutes later, she sauntered up the slope and found Donna in her garden, under the mulberry tree. It was a pretty and thriving arrangement of spice pinks, bleeding hearts, English daisies, ground phlox, and thin little papery poppies. Gladys thought there was very little doubt who would win their Uncle Patrick's five dollars, unless Lucia suddenly decided she needed the money; she was the one with the lupines and foxgloves, big tall showy plants.

''How's that mean old bitch your mother?'' Donna asked.

''*Donna!*''

''Well, she is. Were you there, when she went after Kit?''

''No . . . I heard they'd had a little argument about something. She's in bed now. At least, I think so.''

Donna unwillingly remembered the cry in the night, in what might have been her dream.

''If I were you, I'd go and look,'' she said darkly.

Something in her voice frightened Gladys.

''Will you come with me?''

''No. Catch *me* in that woman's house.'' Donna turned her back and went on wielding Kit's hoe. Nice loose earth would take watering better.

Gladys was back, breathless in five minutes. ''She isn't in her bed and it hasn't been slept in. She's not at Aunt Rosemary's and she promised she'd be there no later than ten o'clock. Oh, who shall we tell? Your father?''

''He's not to be interrupted under any circumstances until at least one o'clock,'' Donna said severely. ''Go call Laddy. He's your brother.''

''I did. He said he thought she was asleep too.''

''Well, where she's concerned, I'm minding my own business,'' Donna said. ''If you want, we'll play some pinochle. She'll turn up.''

Mrs. Mint did turn up. She was found by Philip at three. o'clock in the afternoon, drowned, in her fishpond.

FOURTEEN

He had been rehearsing harangues on the way over.

"Do you realize this child will probably end up on a psychiatrist's couch in twenty years from now wondering what hit her? Do you realize that she'll be terrified for life that any close relationship will explode and blow up in her face? It isn't true, Mrs. Mint, that sticks and stones can break your bones but words can never hurt you. Words are lethal. They can wound mortally. They can kill . . ."

The house was open and, he found, empty, but her car was in the garage.

He stalked about her property purposefully.

". . . for God's sake, why don't you pick someone your own size? It's bad enough terrorizing your own kids, that poor bastard Laddy, and Gladys—who's too good to be true, and I mean that literally—but to leap like a jungle animal on a seven-year-old trusting loving kid . . ."

He noticed the green box of fish food lying on the bank at the end of the pond. He looked down through the still, greenish water and saw the dark drifting shape, face down.

"Good Christ," Philip whispered softly to himself.

Knowing it was useless, he went into the pond, in water almost up to his eyes, and got her out, and tried artificial respiration; her open blue eyes watched him at this task, without any kind of expression. No hope. And no fear. He ceased, feeling the clutch of hysteria. Indecent, interfering like this with a dead body . . .

He went back to his house and called the town police. He found Therese in the hammock, reading, and said, "Trouble next door. Mrs. Mint's dead, drowned—sorry to spring it on you like this, but will you right away take the kids, Gladys too, especially Gladys, in the car and go to the lake with them and don't come back for a while?"

Pale, staring, but instantly responsive, Therese rolled out of the hammock.

Mindon Lake was large and long, sparkling and sailboated, among its pines and birches and hazels. At the Bedford end, a sand beach had been created. There was a little wooden pavilion where hot dogs, hamburgers, and soft drinks could be bought.

Therese saw Kit onto the children's float in the shallow water. The sun was bright and hot and there were a good many people basking; only children braved the cold June water. She watched Donna stroking strongly and confidently out to the far float, Gladys following her, and waited until they both climbed out and waved. She went to the telephone in the pavilion.

Patrick answered.

Philip, he said, had gone off to break it to Laddy Mint.

The police had come, with old Dr. Digger, who was the Bedford coroner as well as Mrs. Mint's own doctor.

Digger had calculated roughly that the body had been in the water at least twelve hours, probably longer.

Rosemary Mint, notified by Philip, had, one, burst out crying; two, said that when Mrs. Mint left her house at close to midnight—the doctor had been held up by an emergency delivery—she was going on and on about having forgotten to feed her fish all day; and, three, that she couldn't at the moment take Gladys, as she was much too ill, indeed temporarily bedridden. Philip said that was all right, the Keanes would keep Gladys until arrangements could be made for her.

"Poor devil was only in her early fifties," Patrick said. "She'd been complaining to Digger about dizzy spells and blackouts. He figured she overbalanced and fell into the pond when one of them hit her. She can't swim, couldn't, rather.

Panicked and drowned." He paused, sighed, and said, "The innocence of it. A summer night, feeding the fish. A country kind of death . . ."

"Where is—where is Mrs. Mint now?"

"At Sable's. Phil says he'll go there later with the Mint kid to go through all that gruesome business, coffins, what kind of lining, what sort of handles."

"I know Philip's probably frantic, but what if anything do I say to the children?"

"He says he'll tell them. Lucia's on hand, doing the dirty job of going through Mrs. Mint's closet to choose something for her to be, Christ, dressed in. Stay there for a while. Are you all right?"

"Knees shaking, and I don't want to cry or they'll see and want to know why. *Poor Mrs. Mint*—"

So much bursting, vigorous life. Doused now.

Feeling cold, she went back to the heat and gaiety of the beach.

Kit jumped off the children's float, waded in, and sat down beside her.

"I saw you in there, on the telephone. You look funny."

"Let's have a root beer," Therese said, and then stared, appalled, at Kit.

Kit's story. ". . . and she fell into the water, and couldn't swim. And she drowned . . ."

The brilliant June air dimmed for a moment.

She felt Kit's small hand on her arm, and heard her say:

"Mrs. Mint's dead . . ."

The words had been spoken with a sort of slow, wondering certainty.

No point in evasion, now. Kit's eyes never left her face.

"Yes, how did you know?"

"I thought it was going to happen," Kit said. "I knew it was going to happen."

She shivered suddenly. Something moved over her face and brow like the shadow of a passing cloud. Then her face closed.

Therese reached for a towel. "You're cold . . ."

"I take it back," Kit said. "I didn't know about—she isn't dead, is she? Is she?"

Dear God, Therese thought, I've fallen into a trap that wasn't

really there at all. Gladys and Donna were now swimming back
to shore. She felt she wasn't going to be able to handle this.
Kit might blurt out anything, Mrs. Mint was dead, she wasn't
dead, Kit knew it was going to happen and/or didn't know
anything about it.

Philip probably had his own theories about approaching,
with his children, the fact of death. She didn't want to interfere.

"Kit, don't say anything either way, not in front of Gladys.
I think we'll go home now, but I have some errands in town
on the way back."

She delayed as long as she could, taking the long way round
back to Bedford. Kit sat silently beside her. Donna and Gladys
chattered in the back seat, glowing with well-being after their
cold swim. She bought ice cream cones for them all.

Kit handed hers back. "I don't want any, thank you." Her
voice was hardly above a whisper. She looked flinching, braced,
and without any color at all.

"Well, then," Therese said, "now that the errands are done
I suppose we'll head home."

Ghastly clothes, Lucia thought, erecting the defense of musing on Mrs. Mint's wardrobe. Anything to stop thinking about
her, in the pond. Her father hadn't said if she was face up or
face down . . .

The closet was immaculately neat, lined in rose-printed
wallpaper, which covered the shelves, too. There was a rose-
printed shoe holder; there were rose-printed hatboxes on the
high shelf.

Something dark, or something cheerful?

Fingering through flowered and plaid cottons, and small-
printed dresses of some nameless slippery fabric, she found
what she supposed was Mrs. Mint's best dress, a lilac silk with
elbow sleeves ending in ruffles and more ruffles around the
neck.

She laid it on the bed and went to the window and looked
out, down toward the fishpond. There was no one there. Only
the trampled flattened grass on the bank, and the little green
box. Had the fish been fed before Mrs. Mint joined them, in
the midnight pond?

She went back and decided against Mrs. Mint's sturdy, well-polished black comfort shoes. Or would there be some sort of blanket, or shroud, covering her legs?

Hurry. The one pair of dress-up shoes, black high-heeled pumps, beige nylons, pink underwear . . . Hurry, hurry, hurry, get out of this sunny silent house.

Laddy Mint made an odd gulping, clicking sound in his throat when Philip, as gently as he could, told him.

He had spent a moment first with Jack Elder, the owner of the garage.

Elder, who resented the fact that Philip gave his trade to his rival Turner, said sourly, "Terrible thing. I hope the kid won't have to take too much time off, we're way behind, jammed with work. Sad, though."

Laddy, who had been working on the engine of a yellow Dodge, walked away from Philip, hands to his face, and went into the dark depths of the big cinder-block garage. Philip stood waiting. There had been a sort of cowering about the boy as Philip walked unwillingly to him. But then, of course, he saw my face, Philip thought, doom coming at him across the big cracked concrete apron. There was a smell of oil and gas mingling with the acrid scent of the Queen Anne's lace pushing through the wire fence near the yellow Dodge.

Laddy came back, dry-eyed, his face peculiarly blank.

Ghastly age, Philip thought. Probably wants to be a kid again, pulling the blankets over his head.

Feeling corny, and like a fake scoutmaster, he told Laddy he was the head of the house, now. There were things to be done, arrangements—had his mother ever expressed any particular desires, about—?

"She was always very sharp about people who had what she called cheapskate funerals," Laddy said in a flat voice. "She had an insurance policy especially for hers."

"Do you want to come with me to Sable's and pick out . . . whatever you think she . . .?"

"No," Laddy said. "I've got to have a little time, Mr. Keane. I think I'll just finish up this job here"—he waved vaguely at the yawning hood of the Dodge—"Would you do it? Would you, Mr. Keane? Then, later, I suppose I'll go on home . . ." He hesitated. "Will they—open her up?"

"No. No autopsy. Digger's signed the death certificate. He's the coroner, you know, besides being her own man. She'd been talking to him about bad dizzy spells.'' Not wanting to poke at shrinking flesh, he offhandedly, ''You didn't hear anything? Any cry?''

''No. But then I'd sleep through my own funeral.'' Realizing what he had said, he went a dull red. Philip gave his shoulder a hard kind squeeze and then walked quickly to his car.

It was late, after eleven. Donna lay in bed, arms locked behind her head, staring at the ceiling. Should she? Shouldn't she?

Gladys was in Kit's bed. Kit was sharing the double bed in the guest room with Therese. A little moaning sound came from Gladys, in her sleep. She had wept a great deal and refused dinner.

Donna got out of bed and, in her blue seersucker pajamas, went downstairs.

The three grownups were in the living room, having a drink and not saying much to each other.

Donna sat down on the living-room step, clasping cold hands in her lap.

''Right while we were in the studio, lapping up champagne,'' Philip said. ''Back to bed, Donna.''

''I thought I ought to tell you,'' Donna said, ''that I had a dream or it wasn't a dream, I don't know—I thought I heard Mrs. Mint crying out, *Laddy,* some time in the night.''

Philip lowered his glass to the table and looked hard at her. Then, he said angrily, because he was tired and shaken:

''For God's sake, Donna, a dream or maybe not a dream—are you trying to accuse the kid of something?''

''I just thought I ought to tell you,'' Donna said stonily.

''Well, if it wasn't a dream, she might have been shouting for help, when she felt herself falling—''

''Why didn't he answer her? Why didn't he find her?''

''He was probably fast asleep, Elder works him like a dog at that garage, or playing his radio—or you might have heard her calling Gladys, the names are alike—''

He paused and glared. ''What the hell am I blathering on about? Look here, Donna, we live in a small town where the favorite sport is gossip. If you go around spreading your dream, or whatever it is, I'll have your hide. You could ruin that boy's life with your fancies." Unforgivably at the moment to Donna, he added, "Mrs. Mint is not a dead doll, murdered with a peach."

Rebuked, Donna stood up ramrod straight. She said, "Don't worry, I won't tell anyone, except"—in an icily fastidious way— "I did tell Kit, after you told us she was dead—I promise," and marched up the stairs to the bed.

Philip emptied his glass. "Perhaps I picked the wrong profession," he said. "Poisoned fish, and dead dolls, or was it poison in the tea, and now a real flesh-and-blood detecting job . . . Rest in peace, Mrs. Mint."

Therese was aware of that strange flickering thing, her mouth opening, lips hesitating, and then suddenly closing.

She had been going to tell Philip about Kit's story, Mrs. Mint in the fishpond. She had forgotten it in the confusion of the evening.

" . . . and he gave her a push. And she fell into the water . . . '

" . . . you're still going on and on about Laddy. I thought that was just a silly idea you had."

She decided not to tell Philip or at least not now. Coincidence, or even an eerie prescience . . . and Kit's world, too, was after all awfully small. If you wanted to write the story of someone's death, there were just so many places to dispose of the body. The old well, the road with the cars going by too fast, often braking with a scream of rubber where Willen's Road met Mindon Lane, at the corner of the Keane property. Or the fishpond.

"All the same," Patrick said, "it surprises me a little, everything being tidied up so easily and casually. From my perusal of your books, Phil, I'd expect an investigation of some kind, police, where was everybody when Mrs. Mint toppled, and so on."

"It's often only on paper that people pursue these matters," Philip said. "There's the cost to the town . . . no witnesses, or if there had been they would have come forward . . . Digger surrounded by middle-aged ladies and no doubt menopaused to death . . . the Mints are old respected stock in Bedford . . . so much simpler to place the whole affair six feet deep. This is theory, but to get back to fact, I hope you are not carried away by Donna's dramatics?''

"No . . . it's just, as I said, that it's all so surprisingly tidy. No material for you at all, in this kind of thing.''

Donna lay awake a long time. She was furious at her father, and with the fury there was a strong lacing of guilt. It had not been fair to Laddy Mint, telling only one half of the story, and leaving out about how Kit had drifted up the terrace steps, sleepwalking, or not sleepwalking, a little after the scream that she could after all have dreamed . . .

Kit, in a towering rage with Mrs. Mint. Would she still be angry, revengeful, in her sleeping state? Just a little push would . . .

In spite of the legend about redheads, Donna had an even, sweet temper. It was dark-haired Kit who, on occasion, stamped and shouted and turned scarlet and shoved and struck out with her fists . . .

Had she told them about the scream because what she was really worried about was Kit's being out, then?

Impossible, ridiculous thought, worse than anything in her father's books.

Kit's story, about the drowning of Mrs. Mint.

And before that, days before, "I think Laddy is going to do something to Mrs. Mint.''

Not Kit, Laddy. Round and round.

Ruin his life. I'll have your hide.

She would make it up to Laddy, to whom she had been unfair, by not saying another word, even to herself, about the night cry. And, of course, she would say nothing to anybody about Kit's night walk. And, after a while, she herself would have forgotten all about it. Wouldn't she?

FIFTEEN

"Rosemary has aged terribly, hasn't she, and I never realized how much poor John's head looks like a pumpkin."

"I was trying to tell Elmer how nice Mrs. Mint looks but I couldn't get a word in edgeways, all he could talk about was his indigestion—"

"Can't have spent more than five dollars at most on that. And the chrysanthemums don't look all that fresh to me."

Patrick Keane, in a corner of the Green Room at Sable's Funeral Home, watched and listened with half-guilty relish. The flower critic, a dumpy woman from Scranton, addressed her thin gray husband. Apparently they were Pennsylvania relatives of Mrs. Mint's, who, if he remembered correctly, was originally from Pittsburgh.

The Green Room was well filled. Friends, townspeople who had known Mrs. Mint and were sympathetic, or curious; and the relatives. Mrs. Mint had been a Moran.

Philip had said, "I'm not going to involve myself in those barbaric rites," and Therese, unusually firmly for her, had said they had to go, if only to put in an appearance, for Laddy and Gladys's sake.

Reversing himself, Philip said to Patrick, "You too then. If you can live at my house and drink my booze and eat my food you can damned well summon up the decency to go along and pay your respects to my neighbor."

Rosemary Mint had risen from her sickbed. Her long red-nosed bony face emerged occasionally from clouds of paper tissues, to receive and acknowledge expressions of grief for the passing of Mrs. Mint.

The thin gray man, examining the flowers his wife had disparaged, said, "Do you suppose she left any money?"

"A little insurance, I guess, and what she got when she sold Mint's, I heard fifteen, twenty thousand dollars. Mint left *her* a twenty-five-thousand insurance policy when he died. And of course she owned the house outright. Might be tidy. Don't get your hopes up. It'll all probably go to the boy. And the girl."

Patrick wondered if Laddy Mint, slaving away at his garage, knew that his stepmother was all that warm, financially speaking.

Laddy stood near the coffin, greeting people as they came in. He wore a dark blue suit and a white shirt and a black tie. The light from a floor lamp touched his crimpy-curly brown hair with gold. He should have looked pathetic, Patrick thought, bracing himself there, beside his dead mother, to represent the Mint family. He didn't look pathetic; he looked expressionless, pink-cheeked, and detached.

Every once in a while, his pale blue eyes would go thoughtfully, studyingly, around the room. Donna had come along over Philip's objections; she didn't want, she said, to hurt Laddy Mint's feelings. She had taken a brief, white look at Mrs. Mint. Made up fit to kill, she thought to herself, and almost burst out into hysterical giggling, right there beside the coffin. Then she slipped out and waited for them in the car.

Therese lifted her eyes from Mrs. Mint's rouged and unreally cheerful face and suddenly saw Patrick in his corner, tall, in his gray suit, his fine face composed and listening, looking like a portrait of a man of another time, painted by Whistler. She felt as if someone had given her a blow across the heart. He must have been aware of her eyes on him; he turned his head and smiled at her.

"Where's Kit? I didn't see her," Laddy said, startling her.

"Oh, she's too young, Laddy—"

"I always thought she was supposed to be so advanced for her age," Laddy said. "My mother always said she was the smartest kid she ever knew."

A memorial sort of statement. For a moment it seemed as

if Mrs. Mint was alive and it was Kit, who was dead.

Therese abruptly changed the subject. "Will you stay on in the house for a while?"

"Don't much like to when there's nobody there. Mr. Keane said he'd keep Glad for a while. I can get a room over the garage, at Elder's, until things are decided."

Gladys Mint was being made much of by the relatives, with many a "poor child" and "poor little girl." She had insisted on wearing a dark dress—"Mother wouldn't have liked a bright color"—and was the very picture of a bereft daughter, red-eyed and brave, with a damp handkerchief balled in her hand, being polite, being sweet, making an effort, with the relatives.

"I suppose Rosemary and John will take her," the dumpy woman said. "Though I always heard it said she didn't like the girl and favored Laddy. But, nearest relatives, they're pretty well stuck with her."

Patrick, who had no particular affection for Gladys Mint, felt very sorry for her, being discussed as merchandise to be disposed of. He quenched his feeling that she was, underneath, enjoying her role. And why not, anyway, if it got her safely through it?

He whispered to her, "Let's go out for a few minutes, and cool off."

"All right." She put her hand in his. "All right, Uncle Patrick."

They stood under a great maple tree in the clean sweet air, away from the smell of roses and carnations and the sharp green odor of ferns.

"I feel so awful that I slept right through it," Gladys said, evidently not eager to be coaxed away from the subject. "I might have been able to help if I could have heard anything."

"Why couldn't you hear anything?" He was mildly curious.

"I wear wax stopples in my ears at night. Mother said it was one of my nervous traits, I'd get over it, but the bull-frogs make horrible noises and keep me awake. They go clonk, clonk, till you think you'll scream. I like the little frogs, in the swamp, in the spring, but I hate the bullfrogs."

Patrick, remembering the bass-fiddle noises coming through the night windows of the studio, said he didn't much like them, either.

Fay MacPherson drove up, stopped her car under the tree, came over to them and patted Gladys's head.

"Sad, sad," she said. She moved closer and kissed Patrick lightly on his bruised jaw. "The living must reunite. These things remind us of it. We must reunite and love each other and keep each other warm."

"Well, yes, but not right here, Fay," Patrick said.

Gladys stared. Then, left out, she went back to her stage, in the Green Room. Going up the porch steps, she began, softly, to cry again.

"Funny kind of rendezvous with you, that woman chooses," Therese said, later, to Patrick.

Fay, without Angus, turned up at Mrs. Mint's funeral. It was a splendid day, ringing with light, the air so blue the rich new green of leaves and grass reflected it.

At breakfast, Patrick had said, "It seems the wrong kind of day to be going to a funeral. Especially if you're in the first car."

Donna, still cruelly stabbed by her conscience, telling on Laddy, again insisted on going. "I'll be company for Gladys. She can't seem to stop crying."

Lucia was relieved to be deputed to stay home and keep an eye on Kit.

Fay caught up with Patrick as he was walking through the long soft grass in the cemetery.

"Poor soul. The Solemn Requiem Mass, most impressive, uplifting—terribly long, wasn't it? But to that good soul, time no longer matters."

She flashed him her sparkling dark glance and added, "I'll be over at the studio sometime soon. I've just written the most delicious chapter about how the great seaman took a friend's sailboat out on Mindon Lake and got caught in a puff of wind and capsized and almost drowned, like many sailors he can't swim—oh, wrong subject, right now, I am sorry."

Gladys Mint, who seemed to have adopted Patrick as a substitute parent, held his hand tightly during the short ceremony at the graveside. Birds sang joyously; a breeze stirred the quaking aspen near the grave and made a delightful water-rushing noise.

". . . May her soul and the souls of all the faithful departed through the mercy of God rest in peace. Amen," said the priest.

Kit was sitting idly on the rope swing, legs dangling to the grass, when the dark girl came across the lawn, from the Mints' house.

She thought she knew who it was. The girl had olive skin and very black, long curly hair with a mysterious fiery red flicker about it when the sun hit it. Her eyes were purple-dark, like plums. At eighteen, she had the body of a ripely grown woman.

"Hello there," she said. "I'm Edie Avanti."

"Yes. I've heard about you."

"I bet you have. I just bet you have, Laddy says you were great buddies with Mrs. Mint." Edie seated herself on the grass beside the swing, arranging her pink voile skirts very carefully. "I'm over there, waiting for Laddy. I must say it's nice, now, to see him any old place and any old time. But I don't like funerals, do you?"

"I don't know. I've never been to one."

"I get a different kind of story from everybody of what happened," Edie said. She leaned close to Kit. "What did happen, Kit? What really happened?"

Kit was silent. She wished Edie Avanti wouldn't put her face so close to hers.

"I mean, you live right next door. You can practically see the pond from here, if it wasn't for those trees, those willows. You'd know if anyone would. Laddy says what a smart kid you are."

Kit wanted to jump off the swing and move away from her, but it seemed rude.

"I was asleep," she said. "It was at night, I think."

"I'll give you a dollar if you'll tell me any little thing you've noticed. Any little funny thing that nobody else would notice."

"I didn't notice anything," Kit said, sliding off the swing. "I'm sorry, I have to go and find my sister Lucia now."

Edie Avanti's temper, volatile at best, burst into flame.

"I'm sick of piddling along with you, you sneaking little bitch!" she screamed, and made a dive for Kit. In her panic, all Kit saw were the fiery eyes and the long terrible brilliant red fingernails. She seized the swing seat, stumbled backwards a few feet, and hurled the seat at her attacker.

The wooden board hit Edie squarely in the center of her forehead. She screamed again, and fell. Kit, to the sound of her own rasping sobs, ran into the house.

Lucia, where was Lucia?

Was Edie dead?

She ran into her father's workroom and lay face down on his old leather sofa.

"Por Dios!" the parrot remarked.

Lucia was in the studio, soaking up Patrick.

The luckiest thing that happened to her, that violent summer, was falling in love with her uncle.

In late July, Joe Bolt, the Powells' cousin, strangled a girl, under water, in Mindon Lake. When she was found, her bathing suit had been pulled down to her waist. All he could say to the police was, "I just felt I had to. I mean, I just had to."

But this had yet to happen. It was the pimple between the hairy untidy black eyebrows that did it, for Lucia. She thought she would die of shame if her superb Uncle Patrick ever saw her with a boy with a pimple between his eyebrows.

She lifted a leather-covered flask and sniffed at the cologne in it. Patrick's grassy, faintly aromatic clean smell. Number Thirteen, the gold letters on the flask said. Chantal. Rue Cambon. Paris.

His clothes were on the battered wire hangers, on a long nail driven into the wall. She fingered the thin white linen shirt and the silk pongee one hung under it, the hazel-colored wool suit he had arrived in, airy, faintly harsh to the touch. Such a nice robe, navy blue with little red fleur-de-lis that seemed to move and vibrate. An oatmeal-colored raw silk tie, another one the color of crushed raspberries, a belt that shone like a fallen chestnut in the sun. Why didn't her father have nice, fascinating things like these?

Money, she supposed. She gathered that Patrick made lots of it. Patrick, she thought—I'll call him that. I'm old enough.

She went to the splashed, chipped square of mirror over the

sink and spent quite a while looking at herself, her shining wet-sand hair silhouetted against the silk of Patrick's robe.

They had politely refused John Mint's offer of "a little, modest collation at our place, a bit of meat and drink."

They had come home, after the funeral, shaken, thirsty, silent in the face of sadness, finality. And there was Edie Avanti, sitting waiting for them on the outside back stairway.

With her strong sense of drama, she had chosen not to wash her face when, after a few moments, she came to and found herself bleeding.

Blood from the wound in her forehead ran into her eyes, down the sides of her nose, onto the white lace bib front of her pink voile dress.

"Oh God, oh, no," Philip said. He saw her first. "I'm going back to the cemetery and jump into an empty grave."

Edie rose, clutching the stair rail, and made a staggering movement. That kid, she screeched, that lousy kid Kit, had pretty near killed her. Hit her with the swing seat. She'd been waiting at Mints' for Laddy to come home from the funeral and saw the kid and she looked lonely so she thought she'd come on over and keep her company for a bit. And the kid had backed off and thrown the swing.

"My father will sue yous blind," she screamed. "Or Laddy will. Just a friendly visit and this is what I get—"

"Where is Kit?" Philip asked in a breathless, savage voice. "Did you hurt her, too?"

"In the house somewhere, I guess, she cut and ran, I could've been dead or alive for all she cared. I never laid a finger on her—"

"*Where in the hell is Lucia?*" Philip roared. "What kind of murdering madhouse do we live in here?"

It was Therese who managed to still the voluble, bleeding girl, cleaned and bandaged what was a cut of several inches across but did not look to be deep, persuaded her to lie down and be quiet until the doctor came. She didn't think the wound was serious, but with threats of suits she wanted to take no chances.

Philip ran up the stairs to Kit and Donna's room. Patrick

was the one who found Kit, facedown on the leather sofa. He picked her up in his arms, kissed her forehead, and said, "Your father's looking for you. Are you all right, Kit?"

Dr. Munson said he thought Edie was fine, nothing serious, but just for safety's sake he'd like an X-ray. On a day that now seemed to be going on forever, Patrick and Therese drove Edie to the Bedford Cottage Hospital, waited, were told that there was no problem, and drove Edie to her house.

The girl was silent now; sullen, drained.

"I suppose I should thank yous," she said, and didn't. She got out of the car and picked her way through a crowd of chickens to the front door of her house. They waited to see her inside.

"If her mother comes out and starts all over again, I'll kill myself," Therese said.

"No problem," Patrick said. His foot went down on the accelerator. The blue Buick shot away, with a noise that outraged the chickens.

To Lucia, Philip said icily, "Live and learn. I left you here, in a position of trust. I wouldn't trust you, any more, to take care of a bowl of goldfish."

"I didn't know, I didn't hear anything, I was out at Mother's studio—"

"What were you doing there?"

"Cleaning it—"

"*Cleaning*—that's something else I have to see to. I will have a few well-chose words to say to you, after I finish with Kit. If that Avanti girl, the Walking Wounded, sues, I'll sell you into white slavery to pay the bill."

Lucia started on a nervous giggle, and then, seeing the rage in her father's eyes, changed it into a little choking noise.

"This, as you will soon find out," Philip said, "is not at all funny."

Kit had told her father, over and over again, that Edie had called her a bitch and come after her and she was frightened and yes, she did throw the swing.

"She was after me with her nails—" Fear and suspense had brought on an attack of hiccups.

"But *why*, Kit?"

She hiccuped. She had told him once, twice. She told him again.

"She wanted to know what really happened to Mrs. Mint. Laddy must have made her . . . I said I didn't know, I was asleep." Tears ran down her face. She reached up a hand to touch his cheek. "I couldn't know what happened, when I was asleep. Could I?"

SIXTEEN

The telephone— which Philip regarded, especially during his working hours, as a mortal enemy—rang six times between nine that morning and one in the afternoon. All the calls, except one for Therese from Johnny Coe, were for Patrick.

Even through the closed workroom door, Philip heard the maddening ringing. And for the first time in days, he had begun working well, his mind racing, inventing. The parrot hated the phone too and each time it rang fell into a passion of noisy distress.

The calls were alternately taken by Donna, Lucia, and Therese, all of whom had to remember that Patrick wasn't there if it was Mrs. Morton. Messages were written on the pad.

He was to call his agent in New York no later than four P.M. It was urgent.

Elaine Bunter wanted him for cocktails and dinner on Thursday.

A Mrs. Ghent desired his presence next weekend at a house-party in East Hampton. "Tell him that I've finally gotten hold of that succulent little English actress he so wanted, the good God knows for what." Therese took this call.

Fay MacPherson urgently wished to discuss with him the performance of *Ghosts* she had seen the night before at the Bedford Country Playhouse.

Philip himself had to take the fifth call. He had surfaced to get another mug of black coffee and there was no one else around at the moment. He was tempted not to answer but the damned thing would ring the house hown.

It was the liquor store. Someone had gotten Patrick's order, telephoned by Lucia, mixed up. Was it a case of Johnny Walker Red Label that Mr. Patrick Keane wanted? Or Black Label?

"Black Label," Philip said, in a spirit of revenge, and slammed the receiver down.

A short time later he summoned Therese to his workroom.

"Look here, Therese, you've got to nail Patrick down and find what his plans are, how long he intends staying. I can't have these distractions. This house is going to pot."

"Why don't you ask him?"

"You're Mag's deputy," Philip said crossly. "Mag would do it, for my sake. Mag wouldn't let things simply lurch along like this from day to day. She'd be organized about it."

"It's awkward," Therese said stubbornly.

"It's awkward for me having the phone going every minute and the house in an uproar, bleeding strangers on the back steps, the kids all suddenly taking leave of their senses, Fay in heat over him and Angus no doubt all set to burn the house down—"

"All right," Therese said. "All *right,* Philip."

In her slicker, she went out to the studio through the heavy rain. Patrick seemed to be well settled in; the studio smelled of freshly brewed coffee. He had wrapped a cone of manila paper around the bare electric bulb and the light was buttercup yellow in the dark day. He sat pensively at his typewriter, reading something he had written; she had heard the tapping as she came through the apple trees. He got up when he saw her at the screen door.

He had not stopped being a severe problem to her. She had thought that after a few days they would be easy together, friends, relatives of a sort, comfortable and casual.

It hadn't happened. His touch still burned her—and he touched her often, fingers on her shoulder, her forearm. At the unexpected sound of his voice, any time, anywhere, there was a sudden sharp knocking of her heart. Yes, go away, Patrick, and quickly.

"I'm sorry to interrupt you at work," she said, "but—"

"This is well timed," Patrick said, too close to her, looking

down at her. Was he generating the heat or was it her own?
"I was just thinking about you, sitting here."

Difficult; she didn't want to sound rude. "Philip's having
an awful time with his work . . ."

He bent and unbuttoned her slicker.

"Take off your coat and stay a while." He peeled it off and
tossed it over the wooden chair. "I'll get you coffee. In a
minute."

He put his arms around her and strongly fitted his body to
hers, with a dancer's precision. He tasted her cheek with his
tongue, kissed her mouth corners lightly, and then her mouth
with concentration and passion. She thought she heard him
say, ". . . now, do you know me?" but she was in an enraging
blaze of delight.

She felt his hand on her bare breasts, fingering, stroking,
tenderly and deliberately.

Stunned, she saw his eyes haze and close. He was kissing
her hair now.

"Lovely . . . I knew you would be," he murmured.
"Lovely . . ."

In suspended time, a splat of rain hit the studio roof. An
apple bough near the door creaked in the wind. Blackberry
brambles scratched against the window screen.

Therese made a little helpless sound and then snatched herself
away, her face flaming. He stood smiling at her, as though he,
as though they both were in some kind of dream.

Then, "You look in shock," Patrick said mildly. "It's only
me, Therese darling. I'll get you your coffee."

She was totally unable, for the moment, to speak. And what
would she say, anyway, that wouldn't sound ridiculous? (How
dare you, sir! Who do you think I am, Mrs. Morton? Or Fay
MacPherson? Or your bloody little succulent English actress?)

Conversationally, over his shoulder as he poured coffee, he
went on, "You've been being so carefully pleasant and cool,
and chummy . . . I don't want at all to have you thinking of
me, in a nice cozy way, as your brother-in-law or your nieces'
uncle. I am a determined, dangerous, raiding male. Bear it in
mind. We will find other occasions for underlining the fact."

Therese recovered part of her voice. "Thanks—no coffee—
the reason I came out is that Philip wants to know what your

plans are and how long you're thinking about staying—"

"You're shaking," Patrick said thoughtfully. "Come here."
He held out his arms.

She took a sharp step backwards.

"If you won't tell me, will you let him know, one way or
the other? He is having a frightful time with his work. In a
way I feel responsible." She hardly knew what she was saying
but the trembling air must be filled with normal, everyday
words. "I'm supposed to be running the house, for Mag. At
the moment, it's not a very tight ship."

He had moved close to her again. "And you think I'm
disturbing the peace, do you, Therese? I'm glad you do."

"I think you're an ordinary, pleasant guest," Therese said
flatly. "But Philip obviously doesn't."

"Tell him," Patrick said, "that I have something to do here
and I have no idea how long it will take me to do it. No—that's
the truth but it will drive him mad—tell him I looked very
huffy and said I knew when I was not wanted and wouldn't
stay more than a few days." He added, "I can always go away
and come back. How long will you be here?"

"Until the end of July—"

"Oh, that's good." He looked at his watch. "I'll take you
to lunch, then we'll both be off Phil's hands for a while."

"Thank you, but I have things to do at the house—washing,
shopping—" She pulled on her slicker and reached for the
handle of the screen door.

"Hurry, Therese," he said, gently mocking. "Hurry—before I help you off with your raincoat again."

She felt his presence, projected, from where he stood inside
the screen door, watching her as she ran through the trees.
"No, no, Patrick." Had she whispered it aloud? Easy, approachable little Therese, always ready to be picked up where
she had been left off, no matter what had happened in between,
no hard feelings. A warm available body, a summer diversion
in this nowhere little Connecticut town far from Patrick's ordinary, extraordinary sphere.

Not for the second time. Ever.

Except for Donna, who was writing her story busily at the

dining-room table, the girls presented a problem on the dark, wet afternoon.

Kit didn't look her jolly, rosy self; her eyes were too large, apprehensive. Therese cut out a rough doll-shaped form for her, out of cardboard, found an old Sears, Roebuck catalogue in Philip's workroom, and set her to cutting out clothes from the catalogue for her doll, dresses, hats, coats . . . "Girdles?" Kit asked, becoming interested. Yes, girdles too. And when the doll had a wardrobe, Kit could furnish her house, chairs and tables and curtains and things, and cut out a supply of pots and dishes and toasters and a refrigerator for her kitchen. The living-room floor rapidly came to resemble a disaster area, but Kit seemed happy and intent.

Gladys, next. No, she didn't want to read. It didn't seem right, the day after her mother . . .

Well, would she help with the shopping? Yes, she would like to. It was so nice, so kind of the Keanes to have her there, she said, that she would like to help with anything at all. Therese found herself wishing Gladys wasn't such a terribly good girl.

"It's only me, Therese darling."

Donna and Kit abandoned their pursuits and came along to shop. Therese diverted them with a long ride around the lake, and a swing through Brookfield Center. It was the second time in a few days that she had tried to stay away from the Keane house as long as possible. The first time, tragically, Mrs. Mint on the bank above the fishpond, dead. This time, ridiculously, Patrick.

It was after five when they got back. Therese said, "Everybody change everything you've got on into something dry," and went up the stairs to her room to follow her own orders. The upstairs hall was dark; she flicked on the light at the landing and heard a faintly surprised sound at the other end of the hall.

She turned, startled, to see Laddy Mint, standing outside the door of Kit and Donna's room. Rather, Donna and Gladys's, at the moment.

He wore the tan coverall he worked in, and a raincoat with soaked shoulders.

"What is it?" Therese asked, the words coming out more

sharply than she had intended, because for a fleeting moment she had been oddly frightened.

He came toward her, the small mouth lifting at the corners into a smile.

"Hello, Mrs. Vane, I was looking for Gladys. She wasn't anywhere downstairs and I thought—"

"She's downstairs now and ought to be right up—Gladys, here's Laddy looking for you."

"I hope you don't mind, Mrs. Vane, about my coming upstairs . . . Glad, Aunt Rosemary called the garage, she couldn't get hold of anyone here, and you're to be ready the day after tomorrow, in the morning. She'll be picking you up then."

On the face of it, a perfectly innocent visit. Philip had probably gone for one of his long afternoon walks and the telephone couldn't be heard, out at the studio.

Nevertheless, she went into the bedroom with the two girls and gave a quick look around. Everything seemed normal, Gladys's bed made with hospital exactitude, Donna's suspiciously lumpy, as though the spread had been merely pulled up over a tumble of sheet and blanket, the white curtains at the casement windows blowing out into the rain and whipping in again.

Why hadn't he just stood at the foot of the stairs and called out, for Gladys? Why had he come up and why had he been standing so still, in the dim hall, outside an empty room?

She shrugged aside the questions; they had more or less grown up together, after all, and were used to moving about each others' houses. The momentary impression she had gotten, of furtiveness, was probably her imagination. It was just that the house had been so dark and echoing with rain, for this time of the day, when it was usually pierced and flooded with sunlight.

She took a hot bath and went into her room and was leisurely dressing—silly, niggling decision: look well, in the long red linen dress, slit to the knees at the sides, or put on any old thing, because this was any old evening?—when Philip called up the stairs, "Hurry, Therese, or your drink will go stale."

She put on the red linen, gave her hair a brisk brushing,

sprayed on perfume, and went defiantly straight-backed down the stairs and into the living room.

Philip had lit a fire and Patrick, in a tattersall shirt and clean chinos, was standing before it, his drink in his hand.

"Good evening, Therese," he said pleasantly. "Come over here and get warm. I like your dress."

"Thank you," Therese said. "It is, yes, it is awfully damp and cold. For June. Has the rain stopped?" She took her glass from Philip's hand and went to look out the window near the Dutch door. "Yes. It's stopped. The roses took an awful beating—"

When she turned, she caught the amused look about his mouth and eyes. She was blushing, she supposed; she was glad that Philip hadn't turned on any lamps, and left the illumination to his fire.

Philip, who in spite of the phone calls had done a solid day's work, and had cut through some underbrush that had been impeding him and sailed through a whole chapter, was in a jovial mood.

"You look awfully good tonight," he said, clinking his glass with hers. "Rain becomes you. I've never seen your color better."

"Thank you, Philip," Therese said, and thought she was going to have to cast about for some new words for her evening's vocabulary.

"Well"—he took a grateful gulp of his martini—"are we celebrating, Patrick? Is this a party? I forgot whether Therese said this was your last night here, or not."

"As far as I'm concerned we're celebrating, and it is a party," Patrick said, "but no, it's not my last night. I've got to go to the Bunters' later in the week and I have a few things to see to. As I told Therese, this morning. You remember, Therese."

Therese said, "I'll go put the baked potatoes in," and as she went through the dining room heard Patrick say cheerfully, "You're lucky you've got such a devoted soul to run the place, Phil. Another woman would be lounging around lapping up drinks and flirting with what are after all two perfectly acceptable men. And to hell with the baked potatoes."

Therese, in the kitchen, managed to find a considerable amount of work to do. This crazy tiptoeing, she thought, is dreadful.

I will not have him force me into being sniffy and spinsterly, I will not bridle like a woman surprised by a pat on the rump on a village street. Because that was really what it amounted to.

And soon he would be gone.

SEVENTEEN

When Gladys temporarily took over Kit's bed, Donna had remembered Kit's story, which she said, that night that seemed so long ago, was under her pillow. The story about Mrs. Mint, drowned, with the fish in her hair.

She looked under the pillow and found nothing there; she thought that Kit had probably taken the half-printed, half-scrawled sheets of yellow paper with her when she was told she would move into Therese's room. Then she forgot the whole matter in the confusion of finding sheets and a blanket for Gladys's bed, and a pillow, and in trying to comfort Gladys while her suitcase—"It isn't really mine, it's Mother's, it *was* Mother's"—was unpacked.

The sight of Laddy Mint at the top of the stairs, standing talking to Therese, reminded her again of Kit's story. As far as she knew Laddy had never, before, come upstairs in their house. She felt a stab of alarm. Someone, after all, had taken Kit's piece of paper, about the quarrel, from under the stone in her garden.

The story about Mrs. Mint was much, much worse.

When she had put on a clean, dry dress and her other pair of sandals, she sent Gladys downstairs to make a pot of cocoa, which was about the only thing Gladys knew how to do, in the kitchen, and beckoned Kit into the bedroom.

"What did you do with your story, Kit, that was under your pillow?"

Kit, who had on the smocked lavender lawn dress which had been Therese's present to her on her arrival, and who looked, with her dark hair that Therese had toweled and brushed dry and her white socks and pumps, like a storybook child, was absorbed at the moment in the pleasure of herself. She still missed her mother, but it was nice in Therese's room, it smelled nice, and it was nice to feel the brush on her hair, and her Aunt Therese's hands, firm but light and swift.

She didn't want to be called back to the story under the pillow, and the night when Donna had first asked her about it, when her knees stung as she lay awake.

"I don't remember," she said.

"Stupid ass!" Donna hissed. "You've got to remember. Laddy Mint was up here, you saw him. Why would he come upstairs? What if he was looking for the story?"

"How would he know about it? Only you did."

"He might know you wrote about the quarrel and he might think you wrote about the—other thing too."

"I don't remember, Donna."

"Think. Think. You'd hit Edie Avanti with the swing, and we'd come back from the funeral, after all, it was only the day before yesterday"—Donna herself was amazed at this—"and you were all right by dinnertime and after dinner we came up here with Therese to switch the beds. Would you have given it to Therese?"

"No . . . maybe I threw it away . . ." The past days had held, for Kit, a good deal of pain and fear and shock. A healing, forgetting process had already started, in her mind, a glossing over and gliding away from terrible things.

Donna was angry and troubled; she wanted to strike Kit, startle the truth out of her. Or maybe Kit really didn't remember. She felt herself sorely burdened with things she wished she didn't know and didn't have to worry about. The cry in the night, the sleepwalking, and now the story. And she had been forbidden to do anything about it, by her father.

"You could ruin that boy's life with your fancies . . ."

And Laddy Mint had the run of the house.

Perhaps it would be better to forget it, look the other way. The summer would go peacefully on, the only dramatic events being small interesting ones, like Lucia being put under house arrest for a week because of not keeping a proper eye on Kit during the funeral.

If nobody said anything and nobody did anything, Laddy would feel safe. If he had anything to feel safe, or unsafe, about, that is. He would have no reason to do anything.

No reason to do anything, to Kit.

But if he found the story, he would have no way of knowing it was written before, and not after, Mrs. Mint was drowned. He might tell on Kit.

There was no father around to scold him and tell him not to ruin *Kit's* life with his fancies.

It came as a great if temporary relief when Gladys called up the stairs to say the cocoa was ready.

Lucia, to save face, gave every sign of strongly resenting her punishment. House arrest, at her age! How silly could you get? She spent a lot of time in her room, half reading and half dreaming. She defiantly skipped several meals. She was coldly polite to her father if and when she spoke to him at all.

"I won't have sullenness, Lucia."

"I am not being sullen. I am being formal."

Actually, she was delighted to be able to spend a whole week in the presence of Patrick without having to worry about his thinking what an unpopular girl she must be, no parties, no friends, no boys.

She watched him constantly, drank in every word he said, had delicious imaginings about being invited to Paris to stay in his apartment. The closest she came to anything personal was to tell him, shyly, daringly, that he had very nice feet.

"Well, thank you," Patrick said. "You might run back to the house and bring me a cold beer while you're on your feet. Speaking of feet."

She not only got him his beer but illegally sliced a great deal of the cold turkey that was being saved for dinner, and made him a huge sandwich.

The world seemed to empty and stop when, in midafternoon, she saw him get into the blue convertible. She went to her room and lay down on her bed and thought about him. It was a hot, still afternoon, after yesterday's cold rain; she drifted, wrapped in Patrick's arms, asleep.

When she woke, she thought that by now he might have come back; and in any case, she hadn't collected his lunch things to wash and put away. She spent a long time on her face and hair and put on a sleeveless white dress, thinking resentfully of Therese's pretty, bare sundresses. When she was sprung, she must buy something lower cut, if she could somehow wring the money out of her father.

There was no tapping, no sound from the studio, but he too might be napping. It would be fun to see him asleep, to stand beside his bed, watching over him, not waking him, but he might sense her there and wake and . . .

But then of course, as she hadn't seen his car in the driveway, he couldn't have come back yet.

Flattened, she opened the screen door. She picked up his plate and glass before she saw the confusion in the corner of the room. She made a half-gasping screaming sound and dropped the plate and glass, both of which landed unharmed on a little thick yellow rug she had brought out for his comfort, from her own room, this morning.

Her mother's sculpture of Kit's head, smashed. A piece with the little short straight nose here, a chunk of hair and forehead there, horrible, real. Part of a small slender shoulder was tilted against the wall. What could have made it fall off the heavy square wooden stand. It didn't look as if it had fallen off. It looked as if someone had taken something heavy and hit it hard.

She had to get out of the studio. There was a feeling in the very air, of darkness, violence, which frightened her badly.

Angus, she thought suddenly as she went swiftly through the trees toward the house. Angus, looking for Fay's book about him. It had been hidden under Kit's shoulders with the green cloth draped about them. She was, somehow, afraid to go back and look to see if the folder was still there, afraid to re-enter the violent air.

But then, there had been that visit of Fay's, in the morning. Lucia, listening from the grape arbor, heard her say:

"Can one disturb the distinguished playwright? For one, two, three delightful minutes? I've another chapter to stash away. And you will give me coffee, won't you? I do like that shirt, pongee, so sensual, sensual to one's fingertips . . ."

"I think you mean sensuous, sensuous, Fay," Patrick said.

Lucia went back, found the folder spilling its contents behind Kit's shoulder, picked it up and wrapped it in the little yellow rug.

Patrick, getting out of his car, saw her still-stricken face.

EIGHTEEN

She rushed to him.

"Something awful, in your studio—Kit's head—"

"Kit's *head*."

Patrick ran, Lucia at his heels. Inside the studio, he stood very still, looking at the hunks and shards and features of the broken head. Then he bent and picked up what Lucia hadn't thought to look for, a rusted crowbar which had lain since time immemorial near the blackberry bushes. It was powdered and flecked with plaster.

"Angus?" Lucia asked.

"We'll see . . ." He knelt and scooped the broken pieces together and covered them with the green cloth. He was just in time. Kit was outside the door, peering in.

"Where's my head?" she asked in mild curiosity.

"Dementia jumped up and knocked it over and broke it," Patrick said. "Don't worry, Mag can do another one. Where's your father, at the house?"

"No. He went to see a policeman, about calibers," Kit said.

"The house isn't empty?"

"Empty? I'm there, Donna's there, and Gladys, and Lucia's here—"

"Therese?"

"She's there."

The question could hardly be asked over the telephone, with the young listening ears about. Patrick got into his car again

111

and drove over to Angus MacPherson's house.

It was two miles from the Keanes', at the end of Willen's Road where it swooped down to lose itself forever in King's Highway. A curiously romantic house for the belligerent bow-legged seaman, pale gray with gray shutters and a water-lilied pond under great swaying poplars. Virginia creeper embroidered the red brick chimneys. Wisteria, old and knotted, hung over the open porch along the front.

Braced for what might be trouble, in vivid physical form, Patrick knocked thunderously at the front door. After a moment, it was opened a cautious inch. He saw Angus's brilliant blue eyes, peering. "For God's sake, you'll have the door off the hinges—"

Then Angus flung the door wide open and beamed absent-mindedly at him.

"Well sent!" he cried. "The right man at the right time! I was just going to have a drop of scotch to my tea. Come in. You'll join me?"

He rubbed his hands together. He seemed to be in a tremendous state of satisfaction.

"Six pages, my lad," he said. "Eighteen hundred words. Calm seas and fair winds."

Patrick paused just inside the front door.

"Were you over at Philip's this afternoon? In the studio?"

He knew the answer before it came. Angus looked too pleased, too contented for a man who had recently committed a senseless and furious attack with a crowbar on a lifeless and helpless opponent.

"No, we might drift over later but—sit down, man, sit down, I hope the tea won't blow your head off, I like it strong—"

He poured Patrick a cup and tilted a bottle of scotch over it.

From overhead, there was a sound of kicking, as at a door, and then screaming.

"Let me out of here," Fay screamed.

Angus leaned back in his chair and sipped his powerfully laced black tea with lip-smacking pleasure. His blue eyes twinkled at Patrick.

"I'll give the wench another hour or so up there," he said. "She went somewhere this morning and wouldn't tell me where she'd been. Some mad tale about looking at petunias in a nursery, I always know when she's lying, her eyes flatten out . . . Take my advice. If you ever marry, or if you marry again, that is, be sure and put a stout lock on the outside of your bedroom door. It's a great convenience, at times.''

He listened to the shouts and screams and kicks with the appreciative air of a man hearing a favorite symphony.

''Over to your place, I think she was heading,'' he said, taking his pipe out of his mouth and pointing the stem at a litter of torn typed-over white paper in the fireplace. ''I bagged six pages this time. Fancy the wench thinking she can write at all. Much less a pack of stuff and nonsense about me.''

He told Patrick three highly entertaining, very ribald stories in a row and offered another cup of tea.

''No thanks,'' Patrick said. ''I don't know if it's the noise from above or this skull-splitting beverage of yours, but I must go.''

''She won't let up,'' Angus said fondly. ''You have to say that for the wench. She never lets up.''

Exactly one hour later, he unlocked the door. Fay plunged downstairs and stood in the center of the living room.

''Who was here? Who were you talking to?''

''Some man trying to collect from me for the Campfire Girls.''

''I heard Patrick. I swear I heard Patrick.''

Angus slapped her face. ''I don't want to hear his name on your lips. I happen to like the fellow but he's not for you.''

Fay moved to the mantel and seized a porcelain candlestick and hurled it at him.

He dodged; it smashed against the wall.

''Next time,'' he said mournfully, ''at least throw something that isn't one of a pair.''

Fay glared at the torn pieces of paper in the fireplace and was glad she managed to say only to herself, and not out loud, thank the Lord for carbon paper.

''Senseless vandalism, I suppose,'' Philip said; but he was very much dismayed.

''Has there been a lot of that about?'' Patrick asked.

They were in the studio. Therese thought the green cloth over the little heap of rubble was unpleasantly like the fake green grass mat flung over the fresh piled earth beside Mrs. Mint's grave.

"Nothing beyond the small-town norm," Philip said.

"As far as senseless goes—" Patrick gestured at a small and delicate sculptured deer, an attenuated cherub with a rose in its hand, a little bear sitting up. "Why Kit? In particular? Why not one of those?"

"What are you saying, Patrick?"

"It looks like some kind of pointed nasty message to Kit about something. Or to you, about her, perhaps."

Philip looked helplessly at Therese. "Do you think there's any point in asking Kit if anything is worrying her?"

"I don't think so," Therese said slowly. "Kit is busy running backwards. I don't blame her. It's Donna I'd ask, if I were you. She's a very sharp observer. And very close to Kit. And she's worried about something, I know."

Donna had had a bad afternoon. She had gone to see the destruction, by herself, and was shocked to her marrow, flinching in vicarious pain.

Philip found her in a tree near the front gate, joylessly eating an orange.

He reached up and clasped her ankle. "A bad business about that head of Kit, Donna. Do you have any ideas about it?"

Silence. Donna bit into her orange and a drop of juice fell stingingly into Philip's eye.

"Donna?"

"I'm not supposed to think, I'm not supposed to say," Donna said, suddenly and breathlessly. Her voice rose. "You'd let him kill her. Not just plaster, *her!* It will be all your fault if he does."

Very slowly, Philip asked, "Exactly what does that mean?"

In her fear and rage, she poured it out, told him everything. Including Kit's sleepwalking, or she had supposed it was sleepwalking—and Kit couldn't have pushed Mrs. Mint in the pond, could she?

Donna's freckles, as she looked down at him, were very large and copper-green on her taut white skin.

"Ridiculous," Philip said.

"But who could ever prove that she did or that she didn't? She'd murdered her doll—she was awfully, terribly mad at

Mrs. Mint—she might just have meant to shove her, not really hurt her, drown her, you know how Kit shoves at me, and even you, too, when she's mad—''

She waited painfully for reassurance. She got it.

"Ridiculous, impossible," Philip said, in a voice of absolute finality.

Telling himself that this was probably all nightmare nonsense, he went to find Therese and asked her to help him to put a few questions to several people. They drove over to Elder's Garage first. Laddy Mint was nowhere in sight.

Elder came lounging out of the shadowy garage.

"Is there something I can do for you? I know Turner's got your trade, but I'm always happy to oblige."

"Is Laddy Mint around?"

"Now that his ma's dead he says his name is Lawrence—he's taking a break in his room. Stairs at the back, feel free."

"You go along to the Avantis and come back and pick me up, Therese . . . I somehow feel you should be armed."

"It's all right," Therese said, and drove off.

It was a minute or so before Laddy Mint responded to his knock at the cheap tan flush door at the top of the iron steps.

Get it over. "Laddy, did you stop at my house this afternoon and destroy something?"

Laddy's pale blue eyes, which had looked sleepy, rapidly cleared. "Destroy what? Why would I do anything like that, Mr. Keane?"

"A bust of Kit, in the studio. It's been smashed."

Again, with explicit bewilderment, Laddy asked, "Why on earth would I do that, Mr. Keane? What reason would I have, smashing up Kit's head?"

Philip had a strange impression of a crouching animal, waiting, listening, heart pounding, in some threatened burrow; not the blue-eyed bereaved young boy looking at him. But he couldn't sort it out, then; he was tired, and he was frightened. He forced himself on. Close this particular file, forever.

"Why? Donna thought or imagined she heard your mother crying out your name, the night she died."

"Donna . . ." The eyes narrowed a little. "Donna!"

"It's a very mixed-up story, but she said that Kit was worried about your mother, afraid that something was going to happen to her, though—'' Christ, this was hard going, but Kit's rubble still stared him in the face. The police would handle this kind of thing much better, but how could he go to the police with his children's possible fantasies. Well, yes, I must admit, Sergeant, that my youngest daughter killed her doll that morning. Cyanide was what she fancied . . .

''. . . thought that you might be in some way responsible, Laddy.''

''Might? You either do something or don't do something, it's not a question of might.'' The words came out like hard little pebbles.

''If there weren't questions, mysteries, perhaps children's imaginings, I wouldn't be standing here talking to you,'' Philip said.

There was a long pause; and then that clicking sound in Laddy's throat he had made when Philip told him about his mother's death.

''Children's imaginings, you said it. Like that Kit taking down private conversations, quarrels, at our house, and Mother hearing about it—in a way that might have been what killed her, she was sick as a dog, about Kit—''

His hands were in his pockets. He stared at Philip's sneakers.

''Come to that, did it ever occur to—Donna, that she might have been calling out to me for help, when someone . . .''

Silence.

Suddenly, heavily, he started to cry.

''That quarrel . . . and now I can't even tell her I was sorry about it. I'll never be able to tell her anything again.''

Philip wanted to pat him on the shoulder but couldn't bring himself to.

''Cheer up,'' he said. ''A long life, good things ahead for you, probably, Laddy. Now I'm off.''

Edie Avanti insolently examined Therese's face, hair, tangerine-colored dress and thong sandals.

''I didn't go nowhere near Keanes' and never touched nothing, including no head, and speaking of heads mine aches me ever since that rotten kid hit me, yous may be hearing from

my father about it, and now if yous don't mind I'll go back
and finish my fingernails.''

When they got back to the house, Philip said to Donna,
Lucia, Therese, and Patrick, ''A public announcement. Cob-
webs removed. Nightmare over.'' His voice was crisp and
cheerful. ''Too bad about the head but that's that, hazards of
life in the countryside, as you know one of my favorite subjects.
Some local lout, probably we'll never know. I was somewhat
of a hero just now. I managed to make a nineteen-year-old kid
burst into tears because he couldn't apologize to his mother.
Because she's dead.''

Later that evening, Patrick said to Therese, ''I think Phil,
for a man who lives a life of crime, displays a singular innocence.''

NINETEEN

Therese, who had finished the dishes, was standing wondering whether to throw away Kit's perfectly good, untouched salad or put it into the refrigerator.

To Patrick, propped against a windowsill, watching her with his searchlight intentness, she said, "What do you mean, innocence?"

He didn't have time to answer. From the dining room, Philip called, "Quick! Everybody hide. The MacPhersons' car is just turning in at the driveway. I can't take any more, today."

Hiding, at the Keanes', was not an unusual procedure. Lured by the shabby, happy house, by handsome clever Philip and attractive Mag, by the lake, so nice for swimming and sailing, by the pretty little town with its oval village green and wineglass elms, friends, relatives, even people they hadn't seen for years sought them out, often arriving unannounced. One couple they had not exchanged a word with for seven years got out of their car and came in to say hello and stayed for three days.

This played havoc with Philip's work; he had long ago established the tradition of everybody simply vanishing. Sometimes it worked; sometimes it didn't. It depended on which side put the greatest stamina into outwaiting the other.

Patrick seized Therese's hand and made a dive for the door to the cellar. He switched out the light, which someone had left on, and they sat down a few steps from the top and listened.

His arm went around her. He put his face into her neck and

began kissing it softly. Her disobedient body was beating with delight. His thumb rested firmly on her pulse as he kissed her again.

"Don't make such a commotion, Therese," he breathed.

In spite of herself, she smiled. His fingers touched and searched her face to find her expression, and lingered at the lifted quivering mouth corners, and he laughed too, in a whisper.

There were footsteps, voices, in the kitchen, close to the cellar door.

"It's very peculiar," Fay said. "A half-full glass of something next to Philip's wing chair, and I've never seen him not empty a drink. And this coffee on the windowsill is still hot. It's as though a plague had suddenly struck the house. Or a ship deserted . . . the *Marie-Celeste* . . . where can they all have gotten to?"

"Perhaps the studio," Angus said. "I'll wander over there and take a look."

"And what is this salad doing on the table all by itself? The dinner dishes are tidied. I'm hungry, hungry for the green things of the earth—" There was the sound of a fork against a plate and a distinct crunching noise; Therese had sliced crisp chilled water chestnuts into the salad.

Her mouth obviously full of the green things of the earth, Fay said, "Get us a drink and we'll both go out and look."

"Well, as the fellow's got a case of Black Label here, I don't suppose he'll mind if we have a drop. Get out the ice, wench. Will he have gotten a check in, I wonder? Yon is expensive scotch. Maybe they've been celebrating and they're stretched out senseless somewhere . . ."

"But then, where are the children?"

As it turned out later, Kit was behind the living-room sofa, Donna was under her bed, and Lucia was in her bedroom closet. Philip was hidden in the angle of the back stairway that led from his workroom to the second floor; he kept a store of books on the windowsill there and found himself perfectly content.

Therese, with a silent determined slither away from Patrick, moved two steps farther down the cellar stairs.

"Speaking of the *Marie-Celeste* . . ." Fay's voice, ponder-

ing. Ice clinked, and there were generous pouring sounds.
" . . . do you suppose that girl, Therese—what an affected
name, I don't believe the Loftuses have any French blood—do
you suppose by now she's sleeping with Philip?"

"Your mind only runs one way, wench."

"Well, you told me not to mention the brother's name,
maybe it's he she's after, I'd assume he's quite well fixed as
far as money is concerned, and objectively speaking, don't
glare at me, he's an absolutely divine sexy creature . . . *I* don't
find her attractive, personally. I don't trust these quiet people
and she couldn't be as quiet as she looks, anyway, that idiot
Johnny Coe has been spending the whole week writing a song
about her. God knows what they were up to, Saturday night.
Let's take our drinks out to the studio."

"I don't want you, now or ever, to go anywhere near that
studio, considering the situation I found the two of you in, the
last time. Go in and sit down on the couch and wait. And try
not, if they do turn up, to have your skirts around your navel."

Their voices faded.

From above her, Patrick asked softly, on the edge of laughter,
"And are you sleeping with Philip, Therese?"

"Naturally." She didn't turn her head but spoke to the air
in front of her. "I'm available to anyone who wants to lay a
hand on me."

There was a silence as sharp as a sting.

She got up and felt her way down the stairs, furiously glad—
for about thirty seconds—that she had hurt him. She could
stand it no longer, his nearness, the smothering dark. If the
car was in the garage, she could open the door on the other
side of the furnace and go out and sit in it.

It was there she climbed in and settled down behind the wheel.
He did not follow her.

Rosemary Mint came to pick up Gladys at exactly 10:30 in
the morning.

Gladys, clean, neat, tense, was sitting in a chair by the
window, her suitcase beside her.

Rosemary, after knocking and being admitted by Therese,
took a long, photographing look around the room. Patrick was

stretched on the sofa in a white terry robe he hadn't changed out of, after his early morning swim at the lake, the robe not covering up much of his long, strong, comely copper legs. There were bowls of roses about which Therese had just cut and arranged. Sunlight fell on Dementia, curled sleeping on the mantelpiece. Someone had left a piece of bread and jam on the arm of a chair.

"Don't expect the likes of this at Mints'—*our* Mints', Gladys. We're a working house. I hope," she said to Therese, "you haven't been spoiling Gladys." When she talked, her mouth snapped open and shut like the fastening on a change purse.

"No, she's been very helpful around the house, as a matter of fact. We'll miss her." She wouldn't, really, but she was sorry for Gladys, watching her aunt's face so warily. Studying a new landscape to learn to live in, poor girl; one distinctly without warmth or gaiety.

"You'll be just up the road, hardly a mile," Donna said, to cheer Gladys up.

Dementia jumped to the floor and Rosemary shrieked. "Don't let that cat come near me; I can't bear cats. As for being up the road, and visiting, I'll thank you to remember my brother's nerves, they're very bad, mostly. I've worked out a schedule to keep Gladys occupied, I don't hold with lying about"—she cast a glance at Patrick's legs and pointedly averted her eyes—"but of course she'll be able to run over here occasionally, if she won't be in the way. Oh, and thank you for having her. Lucky that Laddy fixed himself up, over to the garage. It's going to be a little crowded, at our place. And of course it will be hard on John, at first. Not that I'm particularly well, this cold has prostrated me. But we'll manage. We'll manage. Come along, Gladys."

"Come and kiss me goodbye, Gladys," Patrick said.

She did, dolefully, then picked up her suitcase and followed Rosemary Mint out the front door. Donna went politely along to see them to the car.

"Sing Sing," Patrick said. "San Quentin. Poor kid. You might drive over there once in a while, Therese, and take her out on parole."

He got to his feet, absent-mindedly tightening the sash of his robe about his waist. His manner to her was pleasant and friendly; detached.

My brother-in-law, Therese thought. My nieces' uncle.

"I'll remove myself," Patrick said. "I have to go out to the studio and be interviewed by a girl from the Bedford *Herald*. Remember to look me up, in next week's issue."

TWENTY

"And how is the widow Vane?" Johnny Coe asked eagerly. He was perhaps in his early forties, a peculiar mixture of dapperness and cragginess. He had a little square mustache centered under his nostrils, and dead-blue, late night eyes.

Patrick said chillingly, "If you mean my sister-in-law, Therese, she's fine."

"I'd have been over to see her but she warned me off, says Philip is going crazy trying to finish a book and is a wild animal, will allow no company in the house—well, I've been in the same shape, I understand how he feels."

Patrick had gone to Elaine Bunter's dinner party to give Philip and Therese and the household in general a respite from him. He had politely asked Therese if she would like to come along, it would be informal, a buffet. She had declined with equal politeness, saying she had dinner to cook and that Philip was feeling restless and wanted to take her out for a drink afterwards.

Lucia, from the kitchen window, watched staggered as Patrick got into his car. He wore a white linen suit and white tasseled shoes and looked improbably superb, his face and hands and neck a golden copper color from the sun.

Philip saw him too. "Peacock!" he said.

The dinner party had gone predictably, from the shrimp dip to the cold sliced ham and turkey to Elaine Bunter attacking him fiercely with hot gray eyes and half-bared breasts whenever her husband's back was turned, to the local bon vivant who probably told the same long anecdotes at every Bedford party to the three women who told him they adored his plays to Johnny Coe, urged finally to the piano, and singing, "Oh-oh Oriole" and "Pray Forget Me," this last bringing tears and a meaning look at Patrick to Elaine's eyes.

In a muttered aside to Patrick, Johnny Coe said he'd written a new song, the name of it was "My Therese," but of course he didn't want to sing it here, you know what I mean, old chap, but Patrick would hear it all in good time at the Keanes'.

Patrick talked, watched, and listened, pursuing his usual habit of filing away bits and pieces of dialogue for possible future use; you never knew when they would come in handy.

"And what are you working on now?" a pretty blonde asked him. "A play?"

"Yes. I usually am."

"Can I dare ask what it's about?"

Mainly to amuse and warm himself, he said. "It's a rewrite of an old play of mine. About something that happened here, years ago, and went wrong."

"But it's about men and women, and love, like your other plays?"

"Yes."

People started to dance, to Johnny Coe's piano. The blonde was as good a dancer as Patrick was and he decided to defer his departure for a while. It was after twelve when he looked at his watch and said he must go.

"Oh, no," the blonde wailed. "We're having such fun and every woman here absolutely hates me—besides, I think my husband's upstairs in bed with a friend of ours and you can't very well leave me alone—"

"If I were you, I'd go and amuse myself with her husband," Patrick advised, and added that he was sorry, but he always started work at five in the morning and must get his sleep.

There were no lights on in the Keane house. He got out of the car and stood irresolutely beside it. He had downed a good many drinks at the party, in his boredom, but he had exercised some of them off, and he was wide awake.

The night was very dark; there was no moon. He waited until his eyes adjusted to the darkness and then strolled under the mulberry tree, past Donna's garden, and around to the terrace. The red Dorothy Perkinses floated their fragrance on the air; the pink ones, on the other side of the terrace steps, had no scent. Gladys's hated bullfrog turned up and took over the other, lesser night sounds, the faint rustling of the hickory leaves, a distant bird sleepily cheeping.

He paused for a moment, looking up at the guest-room windows, where Therese lay sleeping.

Faintly smiling to himself, he continued his circle of the house. Down past the mock-orange bush where the roses turned the terrace corner, past the apple tree where Kit's swing hung silently, through a retaining wall on one side and a dry stone wall on the other into a sort of sunken quadrangle, grassy, warm, and protected. To his right, beyond the wall, was a big uptilted meadow that ran, edged on its outer borders with wild roses, blackberry brambles, black alder and larches, to the corner where Willen's Road met Mindon Lane.

The meadow was full of long grass and daisies and devil's paintbrush. Philip had talked, on and off for a number of years, of plowing it up and planting an immense, ambitious garden, corn, tomatoes, every kind of vegetable, but he hadn't yet gotten around to it.

Patrick was halfway through the apple trees on his journey back to the studio when he heard, from what seemed to be the far corner of the meadow where the two roads met, a crackling, something moving among the young trees and underbrush.

It wasn't until then that he realized he had been, in a way, without thinking much about it, patrolling, guarding the Keane house, seeing that all was well and safe.

A night animal, probably, fox or beaver or skunk; or a dog in the mood for mating. It wouldn't hurt to take a look. He was still very much awake, and enjoying the murmurous country night, after the inane clack and clatter of the voices at Elaine Bunter's party.

And he was unable to dismiss, with Philip, most of the childrens' fears and possible fantasies about Mrs. Mint; to brush a lot of uncomfortable matters under the rug. There had been the two very real attacks by enraged females on the unfortunate Kit. And there had been the highly selective and violent wrecking of Kit's head.

The winding driveway was to his left; he went swiftly along it, turned into Mindon Lane and went up the hill to the corner where the sounds had come from. All was still. Then he half saw, half sensed, something in the meadow below, something that might be a shape, a shadow among shadows, moving very slowly toward the far side of the field, toward the house. Not wanting to make crashing sounds in the trees, as the intruder had—if this wasn't after all his imagination, a trick of the darkness—he ran silently down Willen's Road and in at the front lawn gate opening beside Kit's garden.

Cladys Mint felt that she was doing a very terrible thing.

She had chosen the entrance through the meadow because she thought someone, Aunt Rosemary or Uncle John, would rouse in the house on Strawberry Street and get into the car and come roaring after her. The car would brake at the front gate or the driveway, and she would be caught and punished.

It had been an awful day for her. After the pleasures of the Keanes' house, the nice voices, people laughing, and being easily and naturally nice to each other, the deliberately dimmed house on Strawberry Street had seemed to close on her like a trap.

She had been given the small airless room where Rosemary's sister Madge had lain in her bed and slowly died. Everything in the room had been preserved intact, including Madge's clothes in the closet. Gladys had to push them aside to hang up her own clothes. She was not imaginative, but she felt stale sorrow like a smell around her in the bedroom.

Her Uncle John had had a spell of nerves and not even the radio could be played. There had been tough gray round steak for dinner, and watery boiled potatoes. "Don't just stare at your plate, Gladys," Aunt Rosemary said. "We don't serve caviar and champagne for dinner here, we don't live on credit, as those Keanes do, we pay our way, every day." She had broken a willow-patterned dinner plate when she was washing the dishes, had been slapped hard by her aunt, and then both of them were scolded by John Mint, who said couldn't a man have a little peace and quiet in his own house and his nerves would be the death of him if this sort of thing kept up.

When Laddy called, she poured it all out to him on the

telephone. Rosemary was taking a bath and John had retired to bed. She couldn't remember who thought of it first, she or Laddy, but she heard herself saying breathlessly, "Yes, I'm not staying, I can't stand it, I don't care, I know they'll take me in, for a little while, anyway—"

"Make the break now or you're stuck forever," Laddy advised. "Listening to her. Doling out pills for him and pretty soon emptying bedpans, I wouldn't wonder. I'll see if I can fix you up here, the Elders have a spare room they sometimes rent out in summer. Ma Elder is a nice kind of woman. I don't think *they'd* go to law about it . . . that costs money."

She had waited, lying neatly in her bed, until the clock downstairs chimed twelve, and then dressed and packed her clothes and on tiptoe left the sorrow-smelling room and the sleeping house.

She went through the quadrangle and had reached the mock-orange bush when she paused, terrified, hearing something not far away that might be footsteps. Or was it Dementia, prowling? Or black-and-white Margaret, whom the Keanes had kindly adopted?

She intended, if the front door was locked, and it seldom was, to slip into the house the way she had seen Kit going in and out; stand up on the terrace wall and pull herself up to the eaves and slide through one of the open casement windows. She would shush Donna, and Donna would, for one night, certainly, share her bed with her.

After waiting, and listening over the loud flurried beating of her heart, and hearing nothing, she moved again, around the terrace corner toward the steps.

Something swooped, hugely, powerfully, bent and caught and grasped her. She opened her mouth and tried to scream but all the noise she could make was a sort of gasping moan.

An astonished voice, a safe voice, deep and familiar, said, "*Gladys?* What the hell—"

In her relief, she started to cry. He took her out to the studio and they had what she thought of afterwards as a very nice private party. Patrick had a drink and gave her a glass of cold lemonade Lucia had left for him as a nightcap, along with a cheese sandwich. He listened thoughtfully, while she told him about the bedroom, and the plate, and the slap, and her uncle's nerves, and the possibility of a room at the Elders', to be near her brother.

Then he said, "We'll see about everything in the morning. What time do they wake up, at the Mints? When will they miss you? We don't want to start any heart attacks over there."

"About seven, I think."

"Oh God, my sins coming home to roost." Gladys didn't at all know what he meant. "Although it's two hours better than five o'clock. You can sleep here, I'll go over and take the sofa. You won't be frightened?"

"No, I like it here . . . Uncle Patrick."

"Good night, then." He hesitated, then bent and kissed her cheek. "Sleep well, Gladys."

Rosemary Mint was enjoying, with Patrick, having her cake and eating it too. She raged about ungratefulness, sneakiness, outrageous behavior; and was mightily relieved at the same time to be, even if only temporarily, rid of the nuisance and responsibility of having Gladys under her roof.

"After all, the girl's just lost her mother," Patrick said. "And she more or less grew up with the Keanes, I suppose they're a sort of family to her too. Suppose we say a week there, to let her get her bearings back."

Rosemary's change-purse mouth snapped open. "It's all the same to me, if she prefers them to our company." It snapped shut again.

Imagine, she thought, watching him as he went down the cement walk to his car. Imagine dolling yourself up in a white linen suit, and white shoes, at seven o'clock in the morning!

No wonder that ungrateful girl Gladys was spoiled with the fancy living at the Keanes'.

It was with a slight hesitation that he approached Philip's closed workroom door, a little after 7:30; he had a natural disinclination to disturb his brother at his work, particularly in the first freshness of the morning, the first hot coffee, always a promising time at the typewriter. But Gladys, upon whom Philip's eye might fall at any moment, had to be explained.

Philip wasn't at the typewriter. He was standing with his back to Patrick, apparently looking out the window at his other meadow, the one with the big dimple of a pond in its center and Willen's Brook at its boundaries.

The room was untidy and comfortable. No one but Mag was ever allowed to try to put it to rights, and she very seldom. There was a wall of jammed bookshelves, a threadbare, blue-and-ivory Chinese rug that had finally been banished from the living room; an old cracked leather sofa, and Philip's big battered oak desk with the typewriter sitting in its well and manuscript pages, some old, some fresh, littering its surfaces.

The parrot made an unwelcoming sound and flared her eyes red at Patrick. Philip turned and scowled. He looked haggard and not like himself.

"I heard you come in last night and settle on the sofa," he said accusingly. "Couldn't you make it to the studio?"

"The studio was serving as a kind of adolescent nursery."

He told Philip about Gladys. Philip rubbed his eyes and said he supposed she could be fitted in again, for a while.

"Phil—is something bothering you badly, over and above your unwanted guest?"

In an irritated way, turning the question aside, Philip said, "When it comes to that, what the hell are you doing here, anyway? I thought you didn't like the quiet life."

"It grows on you."

Not listening, Philip swept on. "What is this crap about a Mrs. Morton? Don't tell me a man of your age and experience can't handle an importunate woman—"

"I thought writers were supposed to be observant. I have designs on Therese."

"You're not planning anything shabby . . . again?"

"Have you for Christ's sake never made a mistake?" Patrick's voice was savage for a moment. "As far as Jenny goes, I should simply have gone to bed with her, and stayed there, for about three months, and that would have been that—"

"I assume you don't have the same idea, about Therese?"

Patrick went dangerously pale.

"You bloody bastard, do you think I'm applying to *you* for her hand?"

Therese, going with her soft-boiled egg to eat her breakfast on the terrace, heard the enraged voice, loud and clear.

Philip took a long breath. "I'm sorry. I was awake most of the night. You ask if I ever make a mistake. The answer is no, never, I'm always magnificently right about everything, I have a penetrating all-seeing intelligence.'' He sounded tired and bitter. ''God, I miss Mag. I all but called her last night and told her to come home. But then—'' He sighed. ''Children are wild animals. She'd know what they're thinking. Not that your Therese isn't helpful and good—and to get back to her, she's had a tough time, Vane's death on top of your—''

''I want to marry her.''

''Oh, well, then.'' Philip looked a little abashed.

'' —that is, if she ever lets me get near enough to ask her.''

''And Mrs. Morton is—?''

''Mrs. Morton, Angie Morton, is sixty-five. She does split the place in Paris with me. A nice woman; salty. You'd like her.''

For a moment, Philip seemed to forget whatever was troubling him. He looked amused and a little angry.

''Just a cover story for a sort of shopping expedition you were on, here? To see if you still wanted her?''

''Or, the other way round. Or both.''

''You'll stay on then, I suppose, until the matter is settled one way or another.''

''If I'm not really fouling up your work—if that isn't *your* cover story. Otherwise I'll take a room somewhere in town.''

''No, no—in a way, the company is cheering. Get us a Bloody Mary to celebrate your possible entrance into my family. I need it anyway.''

''There's nothing to celebrate yet,'' Patrick said, ''but I will. I think I could use one, too, after sharing the dewy dawn with Rosemary Mint.''

''Call off the dogs,'' Philip said later, to Therese. ''Patrick's staying on for a while, after all. Fellow wheedled it out of me. I'm too soft.''

''I know,'' Therese said. ''He gave me some housekeeping money this morning. Is it all right to take it?''

''Is it all *right?* Are you mad?''

''Good then, we can use it.''

Patrick had come upon her drinking her coffee and leaning

on what she now thought of as his kitchen windowsill, the one closest to the sink.

He said, about Gladys's reappearance, that he was sorry to wish Gladys on her again . . .

"But I thought I could hardly send her back right away to settle down on her Aunt Madge's deathbed."

"It's all right, Patrick. In a way I'm glad to see her doing something big, bad, and disobedient."

He had taken his wallet out and given her two hundred dollars.

"Don't look starchy, Therese, it's not for you, it's for my temporarily penniless brother and my poor starving nieces, and it's a good deal cheaper here than at the Bedford Inn, where it turns out I won't have to go after all."

"Pleasant outcome of what sounded like a fight, in Philip's room." She was unaccountably happy about his staying. She knew it was cross grained and contrary of her, but she had found herself thinking that the house would seem awfully quiet, awfully empty, after Patrick left.

He gave her an appalled look. "You didn't hear it all, I hope?"

"No, just 'You bloody bastard, do you think I'm applying to you for her hand?' "

"The English language," he said thoughtfully, "sometimes depends heavily, for clarity, on what word you emphasize."

She put the money in the pocket of her white shorts.

"By the way, thank you," she said, smiling, and as he watched her what seemed to be a rush of silvery light went over her face, "on behalf of my brother-in-law and for our mutual poor starving nieces."

"That," Patrick said obliquely, and in a way that didn't take her long to perfectly well understand, "was yesterday."

TWENTY-ONE

"The fish," Kit said suddenly. "Has anyone fed them, I wonder?"

Gladys was upstairs, having volunteered to clean what was again Donna's and her room. Donna and Kit sat on the terrace steps feeding bread crumbs to the large black ants and watching fascinated as they trundled their prizes up and down what must seem, to them, the slopes and valleys of the broad stones, mica-glittering in the sun.

"Lucia's in love with Uncle Patrick," Donna said, addressing the ant nearest her.

"They can always eat the weeds and things at the bottom of the pond but I think we should feed them."

"She couldn't possibly marry him, he's old, thirty-five, and he's a blood relative, they might have idiots—besides, he's funny, about Therese, he looks at her . . ."

"Aunt Therese," Kit corrected severely. "Let's go and see if the fish are hungry."

"And she's different, not the way she was when she first came up here. She's—"

Donna couldn't find a word for the soft iridescent bloom that had enveloped her aunt.

"Or maybe it's just her getting better after her pneumonia," she said, consideringly.

"I don't think he's fed them."

"He? Who are you talking about?"

135

"Laddy," Kit said. "I don't like to say his name. I haven't seen him over there, feeding them."

"Honest to God, Kit, you have a one-track mind. Come on, then."

It was strange to see the garage doors closed and padlocked at Mrs. Mint's, the windows tight shut, the house silent. The garden, beaten down by the rain of a few days ago, already looked a little tattered and forlorn.

Donna, with deliberate absent-mindedness, expected at any moment to hear Mrs. Mint fling up a window and cry, "Mind the ground phlox, girls, you're tramping all over them!"

The fishpond was a sheet of milk-blue, in the sun. Kit found the sodden green box of caked fish food on the bank where Mrs. Mint had knelt to feed them.

"Come, little fishies," Kit called in her clear sweet voice. "Here, Mitzi, here Bob, here Water-Baby."

Donna wondered if Kit too, by restoring her routine and feeding her fish, was bringing Mrs. Mint back to life.

"Everything all right?" Laddy asked Gladys, over the telephone.

"Yes . . . Uncle Patrick talked to Rosemary. I can stay here for a week."

"What are you up to? What's everybody doing?"

"I'm cleaning, and Kit and Donna are over at the pond, I saw them out of the window, feeding the fish, I think, the poor hungry things."

"See you're near the phone, around one o'clock. I'll call you again then, I have to speak to Ma Elder on my lunch break, about the room."

Gladys said nervously, "Mr. Keane hates to hear the telephone going all the time when he's working."

"Well, we have only the two of us now, don't we? I'm not deserting you, Glad, don't you worry about that."

He called her at one and said Ma Elder thought her spare room would be free in eight or nine days, after the school teacher occupying it went back to New York.

"Anything exciting going on over there?"

"No . . . Uncle Patrick drove away to New York."

"Ma says she'll know by six whether the teacher's going to

leave for sure, or take the room for another week, so I'll call you back.''

He kept his promise. The teacher wouldn't, after all, make up her mind until tomorrow.

''How is it over there?''

Gladys giggled. ''Honestly, Laddy, you'd think there was an all-day movie going on here, the way you talk.''

Lucia lay on the terrace, on an old army blanket, having a sunbath. Patrick, sitting inside on the kitchen windowsill almost directly over her head, said he had to leave for New York in a few minutes. He was to lunch with a legendary square-jawed New England actress who might, or might not, choose to play the part of Cynthia Appleyard in his *In Case of Love*.

He had thankfully changed out of his tired slept-in white suit into dark gray, with a black-and-white gingham shirt and a knitted tie the color of Donna's hair.

''And what are you going to do today, Therese?''

''Go swimming with Johnny Coe, keep an occasional eye on the kids . . .''

The kids.

Lucia whispered it furiously to herself.

Her father's voice suddenly echoed in her ears. ''I wouldn't trust you, any more, to take care of a bowl of goldfish.''

The pan made a screeching noise as Therese put an eye roast of beef into the oven. She had gone off, earlier, to pay the bill of $146.50 at Mint's, and brought back the roast to have cold, for dinner.

''Let me have your face, for a minute,'' Patrick said, putting two of his fingers under her chin and lifting it. Something about his words, or the way he said them, constricted Lucia's lungs. She found it hard to breathe.

She rolled swiftly over and got to her knees and looked in through the screen from an angle that kept her unseen.

''Therese,'' he said, tasting her name. ''Properly accented, the grave and acute Therese, or no, the other way. I wonder which brother she's after. Such an affected name, I don't believe the Loftuses have any French blood. Objectively speaking, don't glare at me, she's an absolutely divine sexy creature—''

''Wrong. *He* is . . .''

For the first time, she allowed herself fleetingly to think how

peculiarly delightful it would be, to be made love to by this
urbane and articulate man, and by the other man she sensed
beneath the surface, kind and strong.

"Have a nice trip," she said. She looked over his shoulder
at the kitchen clock.

"The roast . . . four pounds, one hour or perhaps a little
over—"

He was standing quietly looking down at her. She was very
still, too, her arms limp and motionless at her sides.

The telephone rang. Neither of them seemed to be disposed
to answer it.

"I'll be back to eat it," Patrick said, "God and the Buick
willing. Goodbye, Therese."

"Bitch," Lucia murmured to the summer air, racing for the
phone, "bitch."

"Let me have your face for a minute . . ."

She was able to catch the two of them, in time. She said,
giggling on a high harsh note, "It's your *boy friend*, Aunt
Therese. He wants to talk to you."

Beau Bower's nice voice; how unreal it sounded. How disturbing to see how Patrick's face superimposed itself on his,
Patrick's brow and mouth and nose and eyes, so that it was
difficult to remember what Beau looked like.

"You remember our friendly neighborhood harridan," Beau
said. This being the editor of *You*, Sally Connaught. He sounded
uncomfortable. "She heard that Keane, Patrick Keane, the
playwright, is staying there, with you, and she wants to fix up
a photographic session there, we're putting a thing together on
theater dresses for the holidays. The models with Keane, at his
typewriter, and so forth—"

Therese said swiftly, "I don't think so, Beau. Actually, he's
frightfully shy. And now, I have a roast I must get back to—"

After his lunch, which was a successful one—she would do
it, she would positively love to do it—Patrick went shopping.
For Philip, he brought back a set of Smollett bound in old
brandy-brown leather. Kit and Donna got new bathing suits,
Lucia a seductive bare sundress. How had he known? She wondered about it, enchanted.

He put Therese's presents on the white table beside her bed, as a surprise.

Lucia, coming out of the bathroom, saw him as he was just leaving Therese's room. She smiled at him and went up the hall to her own room. As soon as she heard him safely downstairs, she went into the guest room to see what he had secretly left there.

There was a plate on the table, holding a large yellow-green hothouse pear blushed with rose on one shining cheek, a round flat box of Brie cheese, and a beautiful little fruit knife, its white porcelain handle painted with tiny ribbon-tied bunches of green and purple grapes. Beside the plate lay a French grammar.

Lucia took the plate and the small blue hard-covered book into her bedroom. Recklessly, (I don't care, I don't *care*), she ate the pear, sampled the cheese and disliked it heartily—throw it away later. She hid the Meissen knife under a tangle of clothes in her bottom bureau drawer. The French grammar could go, along with the cheese, into the garbage can.

"Did you like your presents, Therese?" Patrick asked as she poured him his coffee, the morning sunlight finding lavender and red lights in her straight brown hair. "I must say I've been waiting for, 'Oh, thank you, but you shouldn't have taken the trouble and spent all that money'—"

"What presents?"

He took a thoughtful sip of his coffee. He looked out the window. "I think I'll drink this on the terrace."

Lucia was sitting on the terrace wall, under the hickory tree, wearing her new white pique dress. As he approached her, she stretched out a long leg, lazily.

"Hello, Patrick. Do I look nice?"

He studied her; something about the look in his eyes made her skin feel hot and too tight.

"Very nice," he said, "and not at all like a minor pickpocket." He finished his look at her, then turned away and left her.

TWENTY-TWO

"If you picked five or six flowers, you wouldn't have any garden left," the voice said, above and behind the kneeling Kit.

She shot to her feet and turned and Laddy Mint saw the white naked terror on her face.

She backed away from him and moved her mouth but made no sound. He took two steps toward her and she backed away two more.

"Cat got your tongue? I wonder how it would taste, to that crazy Dementia of yours."

His eyes raked her face, her small taut body. He saw her mouth stretching into an O shape. He didn't want to have her screaming at him, or about his presence on the sunny morning lawn.

"Got to pick up Gladys," he explained, and quickly left her standing, looking frozenly after him as he mounted the slope to the terrace.

He went through the Dutch door into the living room, after a polite single knock. From behind the closed door of Philip Keane's workroom there was the sound of a typewriter in full spate. Donna was alone in the room, sitting on the sofa and eating bread and jam with a glass of milk.

Laddy went over and sat down beside her. There was some bread halfway down her throat that she wasn't sure she could swallow, but she took a big gulp of milk and it worked.

"Hi, Donna. Gladys around? I thought I'd run her over to the room at Ma Elder's, the teacher that has it now has gone to Norwalk for the day to visit her sister."

"Gladys had a toothache and Aunt Therese gave her an aspirin and told her to go to bed for a while . . ."

Conversationally, casually, Laddy said, "Now that we have a chance to talk, somebody said, I forget who, that you thought you dreamed you heard a yell, or scream, from Mother, the night she died—"

Donna looked into his flat light blue eyes and felt that what she would say to him was in some way crucial.

Her voice was as casual as his.

"Oh, but then, she was always yelling at you, wasn't she?" An elderly wisdom came to her rescue. "I used to feel sorry for you, *Laddy* this and *Laddy* that . . ."

Her sympathy brought some color back to his face, which had been very pale. Horrified, she saw tears in his eyes.

"You're a good kid, Donna . . . I know you're not supposed to speak ill of the dead but she did give me a bad time, sometimes . . . and my father too, you know, she made his life hell, why couldn't he do anything right, what kind of a man was he—why not take his best customers to the small-claims court to settle their bills—and when he wanted his drop at the end of the day, yell, yell, you'll rot out your liver, and leave me a poor widow with those two kids of yours—"

He looked as though he was somewhere else, not sitting beside her in the morning-shadowed living room. Donna had a peculiar feeling about him: *I don't know who this is.*

Very gently, as though not to disturb the air, set it in motion, she stood up. "I'll go and see how Gladys is, maybe she's awake now and her tooth is better."

"Where's your aunt?"

"Still in the kitchen, I think."

Laddy found Therese eating her egg at the oak table, musing, between spoonfuls, about what Patrick's presents to her had been and what had happened to them.

Seeing him, she had an immediate sense of invasion and felt guilty about it. He had, after all, just been orphaned; you couldn't expect him to look other than he did, strange and lost and somehow smaller and younger. His eyes were fixed, his small thin-lipped mouth tensed, as though for some reason he was waiting, braced, for other disasters.

"Morning, Mrs. Vane. I just saw Kit working in her garden, down by the gate, we had a nice chat, she's a bright kid, isn't she?"

Why was he staring at her in that odd way? She touched a corner of her mouth to see if there was egg on it.

He took fifteen dollars from his pocket and handed it to her. "This is to help with Gladys's upkeep, while she's here."

She hesitated and then reluctantly took the money.

"I'm sure she won't eat up this much, I'll give you back what's left over."

He stood for a moment, still looking silently at her. She wondered what he was trying to gauge, in her face, in the suspension of her spoon over her eggcup.

Abruptly, he said, "About that head, Kit's statue. Edie did it. I got it out of her finally. She didn't mean any real harm, she has a temper and wanted to get back at Kit for hitting her with the swing, but that'll be the end of it."

"Oh, well then—one thing explained . . ."

"One thing?"

A fly buzzed against the window screen. A robin sang in the young quince tree in the terrace corner.

"Didn't you know this was a house of mysteries, Laddy?" Therese asked brightly. "Who took the last of the cold turkey? Who left all the *new* dirty dishes in the sink?" To her instant regret, she added airily, "To say nothing of who killed who—in Mr. Keane's book, you can hear him banging away at it."

He sighed. "I knew you weren't alone in the house, Mrs. Vane, you didn't have to remind me . . . Funny, all of a sudden, I'm not wanted here. As soon as Gladys is seen to and settled in, I won't trouble you any more."

"That's silly, Laddy." Her back was to him as she washed out her cup at the sink. "It's just that I have to keep the house quiet, during Mr. Keane's working hours."

"But with the noise he's making on the typewriter, he wouldn't hear anything that happened—anyway, out here in the kitchen."

She wasn't sure whether she was hearing some kind of half-formed threat or the peevish complaints of a boy at a troubling age, who felt—quite correctly, as it happened—that his presence was unwelcome.

From the kitchen doorway, Gladys said, "Hello, Laddy, I'm better, my toothache's gone, thank you for being so kind, Aunt Therese."

TWENTY-THREE

What had been a light rasping east wind turned in one afternoon, for Angus MacPherson, into what he considered a near-typhoon.

He finished his day's work and got sourly up from the typewriter. He had had to wrestle with every sentence, and he knew he would have to discard three and a half of the four pages which had been so painfully put down.

Fay was out. Her note, left by the teapot and the can of Darjeeling tea and the bottle of scotch on the kitchen counter informed him that she was shopping in Brookfield Center.

He made his tea, laced it with the scotch, and picked up a copy of the Bedford *Herald*, which he almost never read. Its trivialities might take his mind off the labored pages.

Mrs. Angus MacPherson Gives Reading
of Work in Progress Before Bedford
Women's Book and Garden Club

he read.

"The climax today of a most interesting afternoon was Mrs. MacPherson's reading several chapters from her forthcoming book, *The Murky Sea*, subtitled, *The Myth and the Man*, the subject being our local luminary and internationally famous writer, her husband, Angus MacPherson. It was fascinating indeed to hear about the 'quirks' and the details of daily life

145

one would never expect to discover, a little private peep into the other side of a distinguished man's life. In one hilarious chapter, Mrs. MacPherson tells of a sailing incident on our own Mindon Lake, in the course of which the novelist was almost drowned because . . .''

Angus balled the paper in his fist, crushed and tore at it, threw it in the fireplace and put a match to it. The veins on his temples stood out, blue against the ruddy fair skin.

He thought for a moment of going after her, seizing her in the street or hauling her from whatever store she was shopping in, but then it might look to all the world as if he took seriously this babbling of one idiot to a group of other idiots . . .

Breathing heavily, he gulped his tea and got himself another cup. The telephone rang.

By devilish coincidence, it was his publisher, John Faunt, of Faunt and Faunt, calling from his farm in Newfane Valley, Vermont.

They exchanged civilities and then Faunt said, ''I've just gotten a most peculiar call from Fay. She said she was calling from a telephone booth and thought someone might be following her so I mustn't mind if she talked rather fast. She says she has a life of you almost ready to submit to us and is terrified that someone is trying to steal it or destroy it . . .''

He waited, heard only a thunderous silence, and went on.

''I suppose we'll look at it. She talks about sending it to Coxwain if we're not interested. *The Murky Sea,* she's calling it, *The Myth and the Man.* I'm not sure I quite like the sound of that. If some scurrilous house got hold of it, they might conceivably publish, no matter how bad it is, for the gossip value . . .''

MacPherson was a valuable property, to Faunt and Faunt; John Faunt's elegant Baltimore voice was edged with worry.

Angus found his voice. ''I'll take care of the matter. If by any chance the manuscript reaches you of course you'll send it back to me unread.''

''Of course,'' John Faunt said. ''*I'm* not interested in your failings, old man, or what kind of toothpaste you use, or what happened to all your other marriages.''

During his most recent, rampaging search, she had smiled

mysteriously and said, "It's not in the house, spare yourself the trouble . . ."

He now remembered half overhearing her, talking in the low special voice she used when she was conversing with a man with whom she had been expressly forbidden communication, "—and how's my precious baby? No ants? No dry rot?" He had been absorbed in his own problems at the time and had dismissed it.

It came to him as a matter of absolute certainty that the man she had been talking to was Patrick Keane and that the manuscript, of course, was tucked away at the Keanes'. She went there at least three out of the seven days of every week, to talk, gossip, have tea or a drink with Philip. The Keanes were her closest friends; she could go in and out of their house at will.

He scribbled a note for her and drove to the Keane house. It was sunny and silent and at least temporarily empty. He strode the length and breadth of the house, went upstairs, hurled open closet doors, came down again and prowled Philip's workroom, with its stacked and overflowing bookshelves, and realized that it might take a man the better part of a year to get through the Keane clutter.

No matter.

Philip, coming in thirstily from his long afternoon walk, found him stretched out on the sofa reading one of his birthday Smolletts, in a storm of pipe smoke.

He looked at Angus and grinned. "Make yourself comfortable," he said. "Don't stand on ceremony with me. If you're hunting Fay, she's not here. You're in time for a drink."

"Drink it is, lad, maybe many a drink and dinner, breakfast and lunch." Angus heaved himself to his feet. "I've come to get the wench's literary drivelings, she's got them hidden here somewhere. I will not leave this house without them."

It took Philip a few moments to realize that he was deadly in earnest; that here was a new and frightful obstacle to getting on with his work. It would be like having a caged beast within his walls. Angus assured him that he would bring his typewriter over and settle in for any amount of time until he got what he wanted.

While he mixed martinis in his ginger beer crock, Philip

explained patiently that Fay had brought something or other over, on several occasions—he was damned if he was going to go to the wall for her under these appalling circumstances— but that she had said she wasn't telling anyone where she had put them, just in case Angus did turn out to want them back.

"That's as may be," Angus said. "Fill it to the brim, man, don't skimp, I've had a bad day and now this—well, families being what they are, females being what they are, someone here will know, you can count on that."

"Why don't you just demand it from Fay?"

"I know that wench, she never gives in and she never gives up. She'd regard this pursuit of mine as a great compliment. Where's that fellow Patrick? He'd be a likely one to know."

"Out somewhere, I don't know where." At the sight of Donna, wandering into the living room with a glass of lemonade, his heart leaped hopefully.

No, Donna had no idea where Fay's biography was. She was just about to add that when Fay came over, she went out a lot to the studio, but then she thought, seeing the fierce glare in Angus's blue eyes, that she had better not.

"Well, Kit, then. Get Kit. Ask her. She'll probably know." Philip kept telling himself that this would be a simple matter, after all; someone would know, the offending manuscript would be found, and Angus would roar away with it, to deal with it and Fay as he saw fit.

"I'm sick to my stomach, that's why I'm drinking this lemonade," Donna explained, wanting sympathy.

"Well, go throw up and then go and find Kit. This happens to be an important matter, to Angus."

As it turned out, it happened to be an important matter to a number of other people, too.

Therese was stirring shallots in hot oil and butter for the spaghetti sauce when she heard Patrick's car in the driveway. A slam of the door in the summer silence, his feet running up the back stairway, and then he was in the kitchen, with two huge clinking paper bags.

In the pantry, setting his bottles down on the counter, he recited, "Vodka, gin, vermouth, brandy, Bushmills—it seems to me I remember your suitor Johnny Coe has a fancy for Bushmills, what does Beau Bowers drink?—that ought to do it. There's still plenty of scotch.''

He came out and leaned against his windowsill.

"What's the celebration about?"

"Isn't it madhouse night at the Keanes'? I seem to remember, Saturdays, people appearing from under stones and through cracks in the walls.''

"Oh God, I forgot."

Possibly because of Mrs. Mint's fresh death, or more likely because most of them had converged on Elaine Bunter's buffet dinner, there had been no guests the previous Saturday night.

"In any case I thought it would be nice to have a special windup festival tonight,'' Patrick said. "I think I'll be heading back to New York for a while.''

Therese was skinning a fresh tomato, which she had just taken out of boiling water. Her knife stopped for a minute.

"Oh . . .?"

"I can't really work here, too many temptations and distractions, which is a good enough reason but not of course the real one.''

He moved, came over to her and put his hands on her shoulders.

"That funny silvery light that comes over you when I touch you . . . '' he said. "But about going away, you may not know it and you may not mean it, consciously, but I think you've been punishing me. You have every right to, up to a point. But, then . . .''

"I *haven't!*'' Therese said, the more hotly because it struck her in a flash that he was, possibly, right.

"I'm not good at dangling, and if the punishment is going to continue much longer it might be better at a distance. You have no idea how difficult it is to keep my hands off you. I want you very badly and very soon, Therese, right now as a matter of fact—''

"I at your side," Therese said in a strange faraway voice. "Like a—moorhen with a great splendid peacock, women collapsing prone before your feet . . .''

"Not a moorhen. A dove. My dove. My rest. My home.'' His arms were around her and his face was in her hair. The swinging door of the kitchen was flung open.

"Oh, God, sorry,'' Philip said. "But disaster—another

one—has struck this benighted house. Come and have your drinks and get me off the hook, or we will have Angus as a permanent member of the family."

They went, tranced, into the living room with him. Patrick saluted Therese with his glass and said in a vague voice, "The thing was under Kit's head, but I don't know . . ."

"For Christ's sake, man," Angus snapped, "come back from wherever you've gotten to and join us. You're only ticking over on one cylinder. I assume you've a mind of sorts."

"The head was swept up—"

"Are we in the bathroom now?"

"No, a piece of sculpture, a bust, of Mag's, in the studio. It was on a pedestal. No, there's nothing there now, no folders, nothing."

"This young woman," Angus said, "might make more sense than you do."

"I doubt it," Patrick said.

"I wonder . . ." Therese made a tremendous effort. *My dove. My home.* "I wonder if Lucia . . ."

Lucia had taken out some of her passions and frustrations in a strong revenge against her father, who, while it didn't particularly occur to her, did look a great deal like Patrick.

She cleaned his workroom.

This was done in stages, in the afternoons while he took his walk, or when he was having before-dinner drinks; sometimes she put in a half-hour after dinner.

He had first commanded and then implored her to leave the room alone.

"Mother would want me to see to it," Lucia said firmly. "When it gets to a certain stage, she won't put up with it. It's gotten past that stage. There are great balls of dust and the windows are so dirty you can't see through them. There are bits and pieces of a disgusting dead mouse of Dementia's under the radiator. There are ashes over everything, and Peg's sunflower seeds, the hearth is a mess, there must be two thousand crumpled-up pages in the fireplace—"

He almost lost, in the cleaning hurricane, a whole chapter he had tentatively discarded and now found would fit in nicely. He never did find some invaluable reference material on the destruction which certain musical notes, too high for the human ear to hear, could wreak. The mathematical neatness and precision of his desk, his tidied manuscript and squared-off stack of manila paper, depressed and confused him and made him feel as if he was working in someone's office for somebody else.

In despair, he had said, "I can't quite remember how long the house arrest was to run but it must be over by now. Why don't you call up a friend and get out and see the great world again? Here's some money, you haven't had any lately."

While they waited for her, Lucia was having a wonderful time in Beresford's Drugstore. A new line of cosmetics, Desire Me, had just been added, and she knew the girl behind the counter; she was in Lucia's class at Bedford Senior High School.

There were row upon row of testers: eye make-up, lipsticks, creams, lotions, perfumes and colognes, liquid make-up, powder, after-bath products.

"I want to try everything, Flo," Lucia said. "I mean absolutely everything."

TWENTY-FOUR

Kit stood looking forlornly at her garden.

"If you picked five or six flowers you wouldn't have any garden left . . ."

Horrible Laddy Mint.

She had a thought. She said to Gladys, who was sitting on the stone wall beside her, "I don't suppose it would hurt to take some of the poor plants out of your mother's garden. There's nobody to water and weed them and I could plant them here."

"Go ahead, they're only going to waste," Gladys said with a lofty graciousness. It wasn't any particular fun, having Kit for company, but Donna was up in the bedroom, doubled over on her bed with her cramps, looking white and ill, her freckles very large and green. Gladys wanted to tell Therese, but Donna had said fiercely, "*No*. Don't you dare. It's nothing. It will go away. Leave me alone, I just want to rest and get warm. Or, get me an aspirin."

Mag's cure for most of her children's mild ills was aspirin. Donna took it and drifted off. She slept through the whole thing.

Kit jumped off the wall and picked up her trowel from the grass. "Come on, then, Gladys."

"You go, it's your garden you want to fix up. Therese asked me to watch for the vegetable man out at the end of the drive, on his way home. It's almost time for him now."

Therese had also told her to keep her eye on Kit; but the

vegetable man was usually accompanied by his sixteen-year-old son, and Gladys didn't want the redheaded boy, George, to think her only company was a kid half her age.

"Where's . . . your brother?" Kit asked, trying to make it sound casual.

"He's in Bridgeport all this week and next, taking night classes in engineering."

"Remember, Gladys. No matter who asks. No matter *who*. I'm in Bridgeport all this week and next, taking night classes in engineering."

She had thought it was a little odd, but didn't like to ask questions, particularly when he added, "It has something to do with us, and our future, and I'll tell you about it later. It's a bit of a problem, taking you on, Glad, but then I'd hate to see you go back to that house on Strawberry Street, and your time at the Keanes' will be up soon . . ."

"Don't worry, Laddy, I'll remember—anyone at all."

The choice was delightful. Would she take the pale blue pansies? They were in nice thick clumps. The sweet williams? The bachelor's buttons were tall and would make a show. She knelt on a flat stone that was cooling, now, in the shadows, and thrust her trowel deeply and carefully under a clump of pansies.

One oil-smelling hand clasped her shoulder hard. The other fastened tightly about her mouth and chin. She was lifted and in the space of a second was in the garage; the narrow slit closed on absolute darkness.

"Don't worry," Laddy Mint's voice breathed, somewhere over her head. "Don't make a sound."

She couldn't, with his hand over her mouth, hurting her. She had no thoughts at all, in her infinity of terror.

Laddy carried her up the stairs to the kitchen, kicked the door open, kicked it shut. The windows were closed and the shades were down. She writhed madly.

He went up the inner stairs to his bedroom, closed the door, turned on the light, and put her down on his bed. He held one finger to his lips; his other hand was still over her mouth.

"Sssssshh," he said. "I'm not doing anything *to* you, I'm

rescuing you. There's a tramp around. He's broken into the house and made a nest for himself in the cellar. I thought he might do you harm, if he found you, in the garden. Sometimes these tramps hurt kids, do terrible things to them and then kill them. If I take my hand away, will you be quiet?''

He did; she whispered, "Yes . . .''

"Now I'm going downstairs to make you some hot cocoa, you look awful, I didn't mean to scare you like that, but with him about . . . Promise me you won't make a sound or beat on the door or anything. He may be somewhere in the house, I couldn't check because I wanted to get you out of harm's way first. Don't be scared—there's a lock on the outside of the door. Mother put it there, when I was a kid.''

Kit sat up on the edge of the bed and covered her hot face with her earth-dirtied hands and whimpered to herself. She was shaking all over.

Laddy came back, carrying a cup and saucer. "Here. Drink this. It'll help stop you shaking like.''

She didn't want it; she didn't know how she could get it down.

"Drink it! Then I'll do another quick check and in ten minutes you'll be safe and sound back in your own house, in plenty of time for your dinner.''

Recognizing some sort of bargain being struck, Kit put both hands about the cup and drank the cocoa in shuddering gulps, hardly tasting it.

Laddy sat and watched her. It worked out, like a charm.

She was silent and had stopped trembling. The hot liquid had brought a flush of soft pink to her round cheeks, under the dirt smears and the tear marks. She seemed to be very interested in the plaid pattern of the rug, red and yellow and black.

She fell backward, in slow motion. To see that she slept in greater comfort—at that angle, feet dangling to the floor, back flat on the bed, who knows, she might wake up?—he arranged her legs on the clean white spread.

"Where's Kit?'' Therese asked when Gladys brought the paper bags of fresh green peas and asparagus into the kitchen.

"In her garden, still. I just saw her.''

Gladys was glib; perhaps, after all, she shouldn't have left Kit alone, and it hadn't been worth the risk of the grownups' censure, anyway. Redheaded George had not been on the truck, this evening.

Therese went to look out the kitchen window. Kit wasn't in her garden.

"People all over the lot . . ." she said. "By the way," carefully, "where's Laddy?"

"In Bridgeport, he's taking night classes in engineering, all this week and next week too."

Gladys wondered at the sudden long sigh from Therese, the quick, loose drop of her shoulders, as though she was relieved about something, happy again.

He went to check on his housekeeping; a sort of housekeeping in reverse.

The cellar of the Mint house was composed of the garage, a small room that held the furnace and water heater, and a third, earth-floored room where Mrs. Mint kept her baskets of onions and potatoes and apples. Rough built-in shelves held her preserves and pickles and jams and jellies and relishes.

In the center of the floor was the slab of concrete marking the grave of her German Shepherd Netty, whom she had loved so much she never allowed herself another dog.

Her husband, when he was alive, had occasionally taken shelter from the storms upstairs by retreating to this room. It was lit by a small window set into the cheek of the hill. His old upholstered rocker was still there. Beside it was a stack of newspapers and magazines Mrs. Mint couldn't bring herself to throw away.

The room, now, looked unlike its usual neat cool earth-smelling self: an alien spirit had taken possession of it. One pane of the small window, the center one above the latch, had been broken open. There were cigarette butts scattered around, in their thickest concentration in front of the rocker. A greasy old felt hat lay on top of the pile of newspapers. Emptied cans of methylated spirits lay on the floor and stood on the stone windowsill. The back of the chair was draped in a dirty cotton sheet blanket that had once, in some other aeon, been pink. On a nail driven into the wall hung a raveled dingy brown cardigan with all the buttons missing. A plate by the hat held crusts of stale bread and a hardened, oil-glistening rind of cheese.

He wanted a fresh smell of smoke and spirits. He opened a can and poured it over the earth floor. He lit a cigarette, smoked a little of it, and half crushed it underfoot. No, a tramp would smoke it all the way down; he buried it with his heel. The veils of smoke lay thickly on the still air.

His gaze returned to the dog's grave. He made a clicking sound in his throat.

He got a crowbar and a spade from the tool wall in the garage. With the crowbar, he levered up the concrete slab. He leaned it against the far wall and reached for the spade and began to dig.

There was a faint sound from the doorway. He whirled. The kid couldn't have . . .

Edie stood there, her dark eyes huge, staring.

"What are you digging up the floor for?"

"What the hell are you doing here? How did you know where—"

Edie came into the room and looked around with nostrils flared in distaste. "What a mess. Did your old man leave it this way? I would have thought it would've been cleaned up. It stinks—"

"How did you know I was here?"

"If you want to know, I've been following you, the last few days. I thought you looked funny. I thought maybe there was something I could help you with. I wondered what you were doing on a bicycle, with all those cars and trucks, and your own car at Elder's. I seen you going into the house, but then it stays dark, no lights on—a couple of evenings I waited over on Mint's Hill, and watched, for you to come out but you didn't . . ."

"I don't believe you," he said suddenly. He grasped her arm; his fingers dug into her flesh. "What's up your sleeve?"

Edie's eyes flamed black. She screamed at him, "I've been left before, left too many times, good old Edie, have a good time with her in the hay and then move on to the girls in shirtwaist dresses—I wasn't going to get left again, I thought if I knew what you were up to we'd understand each other, you said you wanted to marry me but I haven't heard anything about it since your old lady flopped into the pond, and I wanted to make sure—''

She stopped, not liking the look in his eyes. She backed away a little.

To Laddy Mint, her face became the face of his mother. Her black eyes turned brilliant blue, her nose lengthened, her dark skin became fair, with rose-splashed cheeks. Bossing, commanding, threatening, deamanding, wanting to know his secrets . . .

''I have someone upstairs I have to get rid of,'' he explained in a mild obedient voice. ''Someone who may have seen me do something . . . although I don't really know whether she did or not. Or whether she's afraid to talk about it for fear I'll get back at her. But, you see, it's been bad enough, wondering, minute to minute, a week or more, whether she'll say something. And then, wondering every day of every month, every year of my life, will she finally think, okay, it's safe, I saw something one night you ought to know about, the night Mrs. Mint drowned in the fishpond . . . She's asleep now, just in case someone came poking and looking before I was ready . . . like in a way you did. So I'd be in the clear, and just have to wait until the next chance. I'd tell them, whoever it was, that I found her here, asleep . . . I was going to have a tramp, the one who broke in here, drown her in Willen's Brook but then, by a bit of good luck, I just happened to notice the dog's grave. No chance of anyone outside seeing me.'' He seemed almost pitifully anxious to confess, to confide. ''And who'd ever think of looking here, in a locked house, the last place she'd want to go into is this house, where she had that terrible quarrel with Mother . . .''

Edie took another step backward. ''Why are yous telling me?''—losing, in her fear, her control of her accent—''Yous shouldn't tell anybody that kind of thing.''

''Because it doesn't matter, now,'' Laddy said. Her scream was stifled in his sudden leap.

TWENTY-FIVE

"What's everybody shouting at me for?" Lucia asked innocently. "No, I have no idea where Fay's book bits are . . . is dinner soon? I'm dying."

She carried a shopping bag full of Desire Me bottles, jars, and tubes. She had put on a whole new, extravagant face at the drugstore, and looked unreal and radiant to her tense and irritated audience.

Patrick got up from his chair and said, "Let's go out on the terrace for a moment, Lucia," his grip on her arm allowing no hanging back.

"Where is it?" he said. "You're in and out of the studio all the time. I haven't . . . ." He paused, and she felt as if his hazel eyes were burning a hole in her face. "Told anyone about your nasty little piece of thievery. I think your father would particularly dislike hearing about it."

"It was for you," she said swiftly. "I didn't want that woman on your neck, interrupting you at your work and falling all over you while she did it. The last few chapters are in Therese's suitcase." She smiled, the first deliberately hard smile of her life. "She's so nice, I suppose, nobody would ever suspect her of any kind of collusion with anybody else. But the big folder, the first one, is over at Mints'. I hid it there, oh, ages ago." She told him where.

From the open top of the Dutch door, Therese called after him as he ran down the steps, "Patrick, will you see if Kit is feeding Mrs. Mint's fish? She's not around.''

Impelled by a sense of domestic urgency—Angus stamping up and down the living room, Philip trying to contain his rage at being invaded, Therese, his own only comfort, taking refuge in the kitchen among her pots and pans—he ran down the slope and past the willows and pond; no Kit, but attend to that in a minute or two.

Nothing immediate to worry about, concerning Kit, with Laddy Mint forty-five miles away, in Bridgeport.

The garage door, he noticed, was slightly ajar. Good, he wouldn't have to break the padlock, as he had been prepared, illegally, to do. He went in and following Lucia's directions turned left, into the furnace room. It was pitch black here and he wished he had provided himself with a flashlight. He had no idea where the light switches or cords were.

The pile of newspapers and magazines she had hidden the folder under should be in the room beyond this. On the threshold of it, he almost fell over something.

The barest suggestion of light coming in at the little window draped by the fir trees sketched Edie Avanti, sprawled on her back, her clothes torn and earth-stained, her eyes closed. His first, stunned thought was that she was dead. He felt for her heart and found the faintest, uncertain flicker which suddenly and surprisingly picked up to a steady throbbing.

There was a torn whispering from her throat. Her eyes opened, full of horror. He bent close to hear the words she was trying to shape.

''. . . upstairs . . . something awful . . .''

''I've got to get you out of here,'' Patrick whispered back.

''. . . no . . . please . . . *upstairs* . . .'' Her eyes were frantic. ''I'll play dead . . . for a bit . . .''

He went back through the furnace room and into the garage and up the stairs. The door at the top was unlocked. He opened it into what he thought must be the kitchen, in total darkness. He bumped into a table and felt with his palm a slick surface, like oilcloth. Something on the table, a bottle or salt-cellar, toppled very loudly.

A swish of a swing door opening. Someone was in the room with him. He heard the other's breathing; heavy.

Without being at all aware of it while he bent over Edie, he had instinctively registered a sense of something alien in the room beyond her, strange soiled smells, along with methyl alcohol and stale tobacco.

He moved his fingers almost silently across the surface of the oilcloth to pick up whatever had fallen over. A bottle would be better than nothing. Was there any chance of a light cord, over the table? He swept the air and could not afford the sound of his own shirt, rustling. The breathing was closer, now. Keep the table between them.

". . . *something awful* . . ."

"Who is it?" he said. Christ, this was, after all, just a little house in the country, sitting on its hill on a June evening, its garden and pond below.

The kitchen vibrated with fear, his own and the other's, which he felt like a physical substance pouring from whoever it was standing three or four feet away from him.

"Mr. Keane," Laddy Mint said in a low voice. "Mr. Patrick Keane . . ."

"Nothing to be scared of," Patrick said soothingly. He thought it as well not to mention Edie's survival, or that he knew anything about Edie, down on the threshold of the earth-floored room.

Where he had seen, now he remembered, a thrown-down spade beyond Edie's tangled black head, and a hole begun in the ground.

Invention came to him out of thin air. "I was just looking for Kit. For God's sake can't we have a light? She's wandered off and this house was always a favorite place of hers—"

"This is private property, Mr. Keane. I'm ordering you to leave. I have a knife—"

Something awful, upstairs. With his ingrained way of listening, sorting out words—tuning his ear to hear, not what was said, but what was meant—he thought, Wouldn't she say, he's upstairs? Laddy's upstairs?

Something awful.

They both plunged at each other at once. The knife went deep into Patrick's left shoulder in a savage downward thrust. Not at first feeling anything, he threw his arms around the slight, thin boy, who at the moment was no match for his furious power. Another wild knife thrust, into his thigh; he caught the wrist and tore the knife away, one part of his mind still shouting, upstairs, upstairs, upstairs . . .

His fist caught Laddy Mint's jaw just below the ear. Laddy fell over a chair and hit the floor and got up slowly. Patrick, behind him, holding him in both arms in an iron grip, stumbled him forward, through the swinging door. There should, there had to be a switch by the door. He found it with one swift hand. The inner stairway went up to the left.

"Jesus, you're hurting me, Mr. Keane, I was just protecting my house like a man should—"

Laddy was almost crying. Patrick propelled him up the stairs to the landing. Three doors opened off it, one with a lock on it.

He turned Laddy around and pinned his shoulders to the wall.

"What are you up to? Up here? Upstairs?"

"She's in the woods," Laddy said, his eyes glistening blue. "Wouldn't you like to know where?"

She. "Patrick, will you see if Kit is feeding Mrs. Mint's fish? She's not around . . ."

Laddy was looking up at him, panting, watching him closely.

"We'd have to have an understanding, if I told you where. Fair's fair. You'd have to leave me out of it—"

"It's too bloody late for bargaining," Patrick said, twisting the lock on the door with one hand and then turning the knob. "I'll lock you in this room until you tell me, and while you're gathering your wits together I will call the police."

He flung open the door, one arm still tight around Laddy. The light was on. Kit slept deeply, quietly, peacefully, on the bed.

Patrick picked her up with his free arm, gave one tremendous shove that sent Laddy flying backward onto the bed, his head crashing against the heavily curtained window over it, backed out of the room and closed and locked the door.

He was horrified to see Kit's pale sleeping face suddenly bloodied, and then realized it was his shoulder, where the knife, he knew now, had gone in deep.

Kit was a dead weight in his arms. She shouldn't be sleeping so hard, through the noise and violence and motion. The hall light showed him his way through the kitchen. He went quickly down the stairs into the garage, feeling the warm blood running down his right leg.

Edie was up now on one elbow. He shifted Kit a little and reached down his hand to her.

"Do you think you can walk if I help you? Just up the slope to the Keanes' house . . ."

Somehow between them she was gotten to her feet.

Therese, standing on the top terrace step looking about for Patrick, waiting for Patrick, saw them first.

Kit's head over his shoulder, and her limp hanging legs. A disheveled dark-haired figure beside him, lurching, stumbling. And blood, so much blood, on them all.

Munson attended first to Kit, with a stomach pump.

"I don't like the look of her, drugged," he said, his thumb gentle on her eyelid. She lay on the living-room sofa, her head on Philip's lap, his arms around her and his frantic face bent close to her.

Laddy had given her two of Mrs. Mint's Seconals in her cocoa.

To Therese, gripping the edge of the mantelpiece to keep herself standing upright, he said curtly, "Bandage this man up as best you can for the moment, I'll attend to him as soon as I'm able. The Avanti girl seems to be coming around—"

From Therese's room, where Edie lay on the bed, came the sound of hysterics.

Gladys, numb with fear—things had been said, odds and ends of things, Laddy's name had been mentioned, she was sure of it—tried to soothe Edie.

"He damned near killed me," Edie screamed at her. "He thought he had—he thought he'd left me for dead—and then he was going to kill her, he was getting her grave ready—"

The terrible words poured down the stairs and into the living room, where Kit was retching and vomiting.

Edie's tears swept over her again, and she croaked, through them, "I can't, I can't. It hurts to cry, it *hurts* . . ."

He. He. Who was *he?*

"I'll get you a glass of water, Edie," Gladys said. She went out of the room and ran down the stairs, out through the dining room and kitchen and down the back steps, away from this bleeding, screaming house. Up Willen's Road to Strawberry Street, run, hurry, before they caught you. Run to Aunt Rosemary and Uncle John, run to your own family.

"I'm all right, Therese,' Patrick said, blanched and sweating with pain, sitting on the edge of the tub. She was trying to combine tenderness with thoroughness—especially difficult when her hands hardly seemed to be working at all—as she washed the two wounds. He kissed the forearm near his throbbing shoulder. "You're the one who looks on the point of collapse. Hurry up with your bandaging and I'll get us both a brandy."

"Brandy?" Johnny Coe appeared, inexplicably, at the open bathroom door. "Did I hear brandy?"

His jovial expression vanished. "Brandy it is," he called over his shoulder as he ran down the stairs. He returned almost instantly with a bottle and three glasses. He poured the brandy. "Triples, I think," he said, and sat down on the toilet and watched the bandaging with the vivid attention of a medical student in an operating theater.

Angus had called the police immediately with Patrick's gasped and unlikely sounding information. He waited for the noise of the siren and looked at his watch. Five minutes, not bad.

At a loss to know how to be useful, he stood in the kitchen listening to what he described to himself as the caterwauling from above.

A happy, grim smile appeared on his face at the thought of Fay, following the instructions in the note he had left her: "I've had to go off suddenly to New York. Meet me at your mother's—be sure you catch the 5:10. I may be a while, but when I do turn up at the old tart's I'll take you out to dinner and then we'll do some constructive drinking here and there, we both need a bit of a fling . . ."

He went up the stairs and into Therese's room and bent over the tossing Edie. With a surprising gentleness in so hard and tough a palm, he stroked her forehead and smoothed back her tangled hair; he found a blanket and put it over her.

"Quiet, lass, quiet." He pulled over a white-painted wooden armchair to the side of the bed and sat down in it "Quiet!" he roared at the top of his lungs.

She drew in a great long breath; and was suddenly, completely silent.

*   *   *

His next task was to turn away descending guests at the front and back doors. Now that everybody was out of danger, he took great glee in his assignment, offering cryptic abrupt statements and saying he had no time to explain further, at the moment.

"You'll be glad to know the Italian trollop will live, but she must have quiet," he said to the Bunters.

To Van Moore, the cartoonist, he put a finger to his lips and then muttered, "Not a sound. Lucky the child slept through the whole mad murdering business."

He liked his next line so much that he used it on two sets of guests. "Away with you now. It's dangerous to get too close to a wounded playwright."

It was too late to do anything about Johnny Coe, who had squirreled himself into the family group.

Dinner had never been served. Therese and Lucia made sandwiches and Johnny Coe was bartender, while Patrick talked to the police in Philip's workroom. Philip was upstairs sitting by Kit's bed, watching her in her peaceful soft natural sleep.

He was mentally composing the agonized, self-castigating letter that must go off to his wife in the morning.

". . . it was the sheerest blind luck that saved Kit, no forethought, no care on my part . . . and of course Patrick could have been killed when he stumbled onto the situation, or blinded, or some ghastly thing by that boy slashing away with his knife in the dark. Now it seems insane that I thought there was a chance in a hundred she'd pushed the woman, not really knowing how disastrous the result would be. And maybe one chance in twenty that Laddy Mint had done it, deliberately. To take care of that one chance in twenty, I thought he of all people would want Kit alive, he showed signs of trying to accuse her and as there were no witnesses, what could ever have been proved, either way?" He wouldn't, he thought, add the line that had just run through his head, "Come back, come back to me, Mag darling . . ."

Lucia, finding Donna in bed earlier wanting to know what all the noise and confusion was about, was unexpectedly delicate and kind with her, when she asked, "What's wrong with *you?* I thought you were more or less Kit's guardian," and Donna told her. "Come along to my room. I have all the necessaries, nothing to it, nothing at all."

Johnny Coe asked wistfully, three or four times, if anyone wouldn't like a little round at the piano to brighten things up, and he had a new song he particularly wanted them to hear.

"Another time," Patrick said kindly, "You'll just start up the parrot. Oh, and Johnny—and another girl."

He disapproved of public lovemaking and contented himself with sitting as close as possible on the sofa to Therese and her warmth, his foot propped up on a chair. Donna sat on his other side, leaning her head on his shoulder, which he took as a compliment; she was a reserved child.

Angus was assured by Philip that he would have his *Murky Sea* early tomorrow. "Now that they've taken away that poor murderous ruined kid . . ."

Gladys, who was only missed after several hours, was found to be at her aunt's and uncle's house. "Something scared her," Rosemary Mint shrilled. "What's going on over there? She won't say."

"Nothing, now." Lucia, who made the call, thought that the Mints might as well have one more quiet night's sleep before the wall fell down on them. Or would the police be arriving there, any minute?

In a case of attempted murder—twice—by a minor, did the relatives have to be present? She had a frightful vision of Rosemary Mint in her rimless glasses and flannelette nightgown and her brother John in withered pajamas, standing in front of some kind of tall desk, with her father's friend Sergeant Hutchinson behind it. And Laddy howling like a dog from some distant cell.

Therese tried to call Mrs. Avanti and tell her that Edie was safe, and would spend the night, and that she had saved her niece Kit's life; but there was no one at home. Perhaps, with poor Edie, a night away from her own bed was not unusual.

Philip, on his way to bed, stopped in front of Patrick, on the sofa, rubbed his tired eyes, and said, very quietly, "Thank you, Pat."

They exchanged their slow warm Keane smiles.

"And good night, Therese. Don't let him sit up too long."

At the somehow lonely sound of his closing door above Patrick said, "He'll miss Mag tonight, especially tonight."

"Terribly . . ."

"I'm more fortunately placed, at the moment . . . come around to my good arm."

She did. Freed and alone, they looked at each other, long and deeply.

"No holds barred, now, Therese?" His arms tightened.

She kept her gaze in his.

"None."

"And not because of Kit?"

"As your brother Philip said to me the other day under other circumstances—are you mad?"

"Hereafter I will expect you to quote me, and not my brother."

"All right. Let me . . ." Therese smiled at him in a way he thought he remembered, but hadn't seen for years, and lifted embracing hands to draw his head down to her. "My sweet Patrick, let me have your face for a minute."